"The Night We Were Together Was A Mistake," Sarah Said Passionately.

But she didn't fool Cody. Or herself. She was afraid of what that night meant after years of waiting and wondering. They had come together with magnetic force. Their bodies had meshed and melded, and hidden yearnings had been stirred and awakened.

"It was inevitable," Cody said. "You and me."

Sarah picked up an ornament, a red glittered ball. "We should try to forget what happened between us, Cody."

He took the ball out of her hand and hooked it on a barren branch of the tree. "The way you forgot about me."

"I never forgot about you, Cody."

He pulled her into his arms, wrapping his hands around her waist, his fingers slipping into the back pockets of her jeans. He brought her even closer and felt her tremble from his touch. His gaze drifted down to her sweet, ripe mouth. "Prove it."

Dear Reader,

The second story of SUITE SECRETS takes place in one of my all-time favorite cities, New Orleans, Louisiana. Can you tell I love to write about places I know and love? There's so much history and charm there, and I couldn't set a story in New Orleans without incorporating the amazing efforts from people around the world to rebuild the city and make it as it once was. You'll see how our heroine, country singer Sarah Rose, makes a difference in a town that is progressing but still needs so much help.

Christmastime, goodwill and lost love all play a role in this story of two childhood sweethearts who are unlikely to ever find their way back to each other. Sexy security expert Cody Landon is back in Sarah's life to make her see what she missed out on, but he never expected to find Sarah more innocent than guilty of the charges he'd clung to when she'd walked out on him.

I was lucky to have married my first love, but how many of us wish we could have had a second chance at a lost love?

Stroll the streets of New Orleans, hear the Christmas bells ring and stop in at Café du Monde with me for a simmering cup of café au lait and a yummy beignet.

Good times are to be had by all!

Enjoy!

Charlene

DO NOT DISTURB UNTIL CHRISTMAS

CHARLENE SANDS

Published by Silhouette Books

America's Publisher of Contemporary Romance

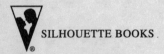 SILHOUETTE BOOKS

ISBN-13: 978-0-373-76906-3
ISBN-10:   0-373-76906-7

DO NOT DISTURB UNTIL CHRISTMAS

Copyright © 2008 by Charlene Swink

Books by Charlene Sands

Silhouette Desire

Like Lightning #1668
Heiress Beware #1729
Bunking Down with the Boss #1746
Fortune's Vengeful Groom #1783
Between the CEO's Sheets #1805
*Five-Star Cowboy #1889
*Do Not Disturb Until Christmas #1906

Harlequin Historical

The Law and Kate Malone #646
Winning Jenna's Heart #662
The Courting of Widow Shaw #710
Renegade Wife #789
Abducted at the Altar #816

*Suite Secrets

CHARLENE SANDS

resides in Southern California with her husband, high school sweetheart and best friend, Don. Proudly, they boast that their children, Jason and Nikki have earned their college degrees. The "empty nesters" now have two cats that have taken over the house.

Charlene has written twenty-five romances and is the recipient of the 2006 National Readers' Choice Award, the 2007 Cataromance Reviewer's Choice Award and recently has been nominated in two categories for the Booksellers Best Award. When not writing, she enjoys sunny California days, Pacific beaches and sitting down with a good book.

She blogs regularly on the all-western site at www.petticoatsandpistols.com and you can also find her at www.myspace.com/charlenesands.

Charlene invites you to visit her Web site at www.charlenesands.com to enter her contests and see what's new.

Special heartfelt thanks to my friend Jim Mona,
a musician and band manager with flair who has
helped me with the behind-the-scenes writing of this
story. And to his wife and my dearest friend,
Robin Rose, whose name I unabashedly stole for my
country star character. To Jake Kale, my New Orleans
(Tulane) connection! Thanks for all the information and
your help with this story. I love you all!

And to my wonderful editor, Diana Ventimiglia,
who is always there to help. You're the best
and I thank you with my whole heart!

One

The scent of hot, fresh coffee called to him from the kitchen of his penthouse suite in the Tempest Hotel, New Orleans. Code Landon walked over to the coffeemaker and poured himself a mug. Thick, mudlike brew, just the way he liked it, slid down his throat, warming him instantly from the cold Louisiana day. He strolled over to the long L-shaped sofa and sat down. Sipping coffee, he picked up the television remote and hit the power button. The widescreen bleeped on, bringing bright hues to Code's parlor and lighting up the room. He channel surfed, put his boots up on the coffee table and leaned back.

Sarah Rose's face appeared on the screen, fifty-two inches of green eyes, soft features and auburn curls. Code took a sharp breath. His heart pounded. He whipped his boots off the table and sat ramrod straight, listening to Sarah's interview.

"My work for the Dream Foundation is very important to me. I'm thrilled to be here in New Orleans and thank the people at Tempest for allowing me the opportunity. This is a great city. We want everyone to work together to rebuild homes for the most needy. No child should be without shelter and a place to call home."

The female interviewer stood beside Sarah, holding the microphone very close to her face. "You're a country superstar now, but you came from humble beginnings, I understand. Is that what drives your charitable work?"

"Yes, I think so. My mother was left with three children to raise and a houseful of bills. I remember that terrible fear as a young girl, thinking we might lose our home any day. No child should live with those frightening thoughts. And because of a natural catastrophe, many people here have already lost their homes. They need our help."

Sarah took it all in stride. She'd been in the limelight most of her adult life. She could handle the press, Code thought. She'd been through a scandal or two earlier in her career. Linked to playboys and athletes, the rumor mills had churned and churned about love triangles and breakups until Code couldn't take hearing about it any more. He'd turn the television off at the mention of Sarah's name. He'd read headlines in tabloids until he learned to ignore them. He'd managed to block out the public Sarah Rose from his mind for the most part, but it was the private girl that he remembered—that had stayed with him all these years.

They'd been deeply in love in high school. He thought he'd found the girl of his dreams, the one and only girl he'd ever want. God, he'd loved her like no tomorrow. But Sarah had plans that didn't include him. She wanted out of Barker, Texas, at all costs. And when the first opportunity had come, she'd packed her bags and left her hometown, leaving him high and dry and completely heartbroken.

It wasn't too long after that Sarah became America's newest female country-western artist, a woman whose concerts earned her big bucks. She raised money for charity. She had small movie roles. She got just what she'd wanted in life.

Code had never gotten over Sarah—the way he'd loved her so deeply and how she'd betrayed him for her career. It had taken him years to figure out that he couldn't move on with his life until he purged her from his system. But he wanted more than that now.

He wanted revenge.

He'd tracked her down at Tempest West in Arizona weeks ago and seduced her. They'd had a brief fling, and Code wanted it to end there and then, but he was drawn to Sarah in ways he couldn't name. He wasn't through with her yet.

His company, Landon Security Agency, had a contract with Tempest Hotels. The timing was perfect; while Sarah was performing here, he would oversee his team's work revamping the hotel's security system. Brock Tyler, owner of the hotel and Code's best friend, had seen clear through his guise but Code didn't care what anyone thought at this point. He had a right to insinuate himself into Sarah's life.

She owed him, and the payback would be sweet.

"Damn it," he said, pushing the power button off. He got up from the sofa, wondering what the hell he'd been waiting for, a personal invitation from Sarah to resume the fling they'd started in Arizona?

Code showered and changed into an Yves Saint Laurent jacket and black trousers, and slipped his feet into calfskin Ferragamo shoes. A quick comb to his thick hair kept the locks from falling onto his forehead, and a pat of cologne finished off his grooming. Satisfied with the cleaned-up version of Code Landon, he strode out the front door with one thing on his mind. Getting back at Sarah Rose for all the heartache she'd caused him.

* * *

"C-Code? W-what are you doing here?" Stunned, Sarah leaned against the doorjamb of her penthouse suite, facing Code Landon. He was the last person she thought she'd see in New Orleans, much less standing at her door. She'd expected room service, for heaven's sake.

She continued to stare as an unwelcome flash of warmth surged through her system. She battled not to let his sudden appearance and those piercing, dark-blue eyes get to her. Wearing black from head to toe in expensive attire, he was as devilishly handsome as they come. But seeing him dressed like a man of success and power was a good reminder of how much he'd changed since they'd known each other in their younger days.

One side of his mouth cocked up in a slight smile. "If I didn't know better, I'd guess you didn't want me here."

She didn't. She thought they'd put their feelings to rest in Arizona. They'd made tender and tumultuous love, a culmination of years of wondering, yearning and heartache. It had been bittersweet yet wonderful, and all Sarah had hoped for when she'd dreamt of making love to Code.

But why was he here now?

She couldn't deal with the myriad emotions swirling through her stomach seeing Code again.

She'd been keeping a hectic pace with interviews, rehearsals and touring the ninth ward, or as the locals called it, the Mighty Nine, and all of it led to the place Sarah wanted to help the most, the area desolated by Hurricane Katrina. Seeing the city's destruction firsthand had put her in a melancholy mood lately. She needed to keep her focus and raise as much money as she could. Code's appearance today could only complicate matters.

"I'm...sorry. My mama taught me better manners. But I am surprised to see you here. Did you want something?"

Code blinked slowly, revealing thick dark lashes and tiny lines around the corners of his eyes that appealed to her in a dozen different ways. "That's a loaded question, babe."

The endearment stayed with her as she combated her innermost feelings.

"Actually, I'm here on business," he explained finally.

"Oh."

"I came to check out your setup here. While you're on Tempest property, my company is responsible for your safety." Code glanced past her into the suite. "Are we having this conversation in your doorway?"

"No, no. Come inside," she said and allowed him entrance. As he walked past her, brushing her arm, she caught a faint whiff of his cologne, the same musky scent that had lingered on her skin after their night between the sheets.

"I'm perfectly safe here in the hotel. My manager takes me wherever I need to go, and if I leave the premises, I have a bodyguard."

"You were attacked while up on stage in Nashville."

He turned to her just as blood drained from her face. She couldn't conceal her discomfort, the memory never far from her mind. A crazed fan had jumped on stage and rushed at her with such force that he'd knocked her down. She'd been startled and frightened, and she'd never forget that one moment when the man had been upon her. She still recalled his insane rumblings in her ear.

A security officer had apprehended the fan and taken him away, but it was Robert, her manager, who had calmed her. He'd cosseted and comforted her, making sure she hadn't been injured in any way. For all his flaws, Robert had come through then, protecting her and giving her the option to cancel the rest of the show. She'd never forget his concern and compassion. After an hour of his soothing talk, she'd made the decision to continue with her performance, and the fans had greeted her with warmth and kindness, giving her a standing ovation at the end.

"How did you hear about that?"

Code cocked a corner of his mouth upward.

"Who didn't hear about it? You made headlines. The whole incident landed on YouTube. Besides, it's my job to know these things."

"It's your *job?*" He made it seem as though he was worried about future employment when they both knew that his company branched out to every corner of the country. She'd read about him on the Internet and in *High Tech Today*. The magazine article depicted the Landon Security Agency as the fastest growing, most innovative company of its kind. He and his father had developed some new type of sensor device that they'd patented and sold to the government for millions.

He wasn't a mere bodyguard. Far from it, yet he'd come from humble beginnings, too. He'd taken the lead from his father's military training and learned the security business from the ground up. His life had followed the American Dream to the letter just as much as hers had, maybe more. Her talent was a gift, not a honed skill born of hard work and gritty perseverance.

"I find that hard to believe, Code."

"I'm doing Brock a favor, Sarah. He asked me to oversee things while I'm here. And you're the big draw to the hotel during the holiday season. I'm just making sure his interests are secure."

Sarah didn't believe him, but there wasn't much she could do about it other than throw him out of her suite.

"Okay, do what needs doing." She wanted to add, *then leave.*

But Sarah didn't really want Code to leave. That was the problem. In her heart of hearts, she wanted Code Landon to stay. There was so much heartache between them. Sarah had run off to pursue her career, abandoning him and their love.

She'd met Robert Gillespie when he'd seen her perform at the Barker County Fair. He'd offered her a way out of the desolate life her family led and Sarah hadn't really had a choice in the matter. Though Code would never see it that way, she'd left Barker, Texas, with nothing but the best of intentions.

Sarah peered into Code's unreadable melt-your-heart eyes. Tingles of awareness crept up and down her limbs when Code removed his jacket and tossed it on the sofa's edge. Sarah whirled around, her way of dismissing him. All she'd wanted to do tonight was to get some rest. The bedroom beckoned, but she wouldn't dare entertain the thought. If Code followed her inside, she wouldn't have the willpower to deny him.

And they'd make another mistake.

Like the one they'd made in Arizona.

Code uttered a quiet oath when Sarah turned her back on him. He had no use for ambitious, callous females: prima donnas who always got what they wanted, no matter the cost. But he saw something flicker in her eyes for one unguarded second. She was an actress of sorts, and that one quick blink squashed her air of indifference toward him.

Sarah wasn't as immune to him as she let on.

He went about inspecting her enormous penthouse suite, giving the place a good examination and double-checking what his team had already put into place for security.

There were hidden cameras in the hallways and corners outside the suite that were classic Landon surveillance, and half a dozen visible cameras which served as an obvious deterrent. All fed into Landon's security center, located on the floor below. The penthouse suites had their own private keycard elevators and a guard posted, so no one could really get by unnoticed.

Code knew his team was top-notch. He didn't need to see their work firsthand. Sarah wasn't in any danger. He'd come here for a different reason and had only used her security as an excuse.

Code finished examining the suite, lingering one minute in her massive bedroom, eyeing the rose-colored bedspread and satin sheets turned down on the bed. The room smelled of her, the sweetly innocent scent of fresh, ripe strawberries.

Code remembered that scent from his youth.

After kissing her into oblivion, their passion stymied by scruples and honor, he would walk away from her stained by a strawberry imprint that remained on his clothes, his mouth and his memory.

He walked into the sitting room and immediately came up short. Sarah hummed a melodic tune while placing a little wax soldier ornament on the Christmas tree. With her back toward him, she didn't know he was watching her. She fingered the delicate figurine before carefully finding a branch to hang the ornament on. She gave utmost attention to her task, the melody she softly hummed carrying across the room and bringing an odd sense of peace.

Wordlessly, Code strode over and stood beside her, picked up an ornament, this one an angel of white with a golden halo, and hung it on a branch. "It's a little early for Christmas, isn't it?" he asked quietly.

Sarah's eyes filled with regret. "No. I have so many to make up for, Code."

Code looked at her standing there, all alone decorating a Christmas tree weeks before it was deemed time, wearing faded designer jeans he knew cost a bundle and a simple white sweater, her wispy auburn tendrils falling out of a silver clip. Something slammed into his gut. "Want some help?"

Sarah's eyes grew beautifully wide. "You want to help me decorate the tree?"

Code nodded. "Seems to me, it's more fun when you don't do it alone."

When she hesitated, he added, "Or we can talk about what happened between us in Arizona."

Sarah blinked and then shoved an ornament in his hand. "Decorate, Code. After we do these, I've got five more boxes to get through."

Code took a better look at the boxes on the floor filled with an array of balls, homemade and hand-painted ornaments, many with inscriptions on them, and realized that these were gifts from her fans.

"You have eight boxes of ornaments?"

"Like I said, I have years of Christmases to make up for." She smiled and glanced down at the boxes. "Want to take back your offer?"

He shook his head. "I don't run from a challenge, babe. You should know that about me."

Sarah placed a brass reindeer ornament on the tree. "It's nice of you to share that information," she said lightly, eyeing her work.

"Consider that a warning," Code said, his tone serious. He meant it.

Sarah slanted him a puzzled look, their eyes meeting. "What are you saying, Code? That you consider *me* a challenge?"

He put another ornament on the tree, the slight hint of strawberries staying with him as he refused Sarah an answer.

Sarah set down the metal hook she was about to snag onto an ornament and stepped away from the tree. "Code, can we just enjoy spending this time together decorating my tree without bringing up the past?"

"You don't like reminders of the past, do you, Sarah?"

Resentment swirled in his gut. He'd thought he was over her, until Arizona. Then he realized he still had demons to chase, and Sarah was a huge part of that.

Her life really began when she had her first number-one hit at the age of nineteen, just six months after leaving him. The hit songs kept coming but her letters to him hadn't. He'd only received one, then all contact between them stopped shortly after her first big success. Code remembered feeling left out in the cold, waiting for a woman who had moved on without him.

He'd never forgive her for that.

"There's no use in it," she said with a resigned shrug.

"We can't ignore Arizona," Code said, watching her eyes flicker at the mention of their lovemaking.

"I think we can," she said, but he knew by the mellow, dewy look in her eyes that she was lying.

"It wasn't a fluke, Sarah."

"It was a mistake," she said passionately, but she didn't fool him.

She was afraid of what that night meant after years of waiting and wondering. They had come together with magnetic force. Their bodies had meshed and melded, and hidden yearnings had been stirred and awakened. Sarah had given way to powerful orgasms and Code had watched her with awe, riding those waves of pleasure. He'd joined her and they'd come home together, climaxing in unison.

"It was inevitable. You and me."

Sarah picked up an ornament, a red glittered ball with the embellished words, "From your biggest fan, Joellen," and a picture of the smiling young girl dead center. She stared at the orb for a moment as she gathered her thoughts and then shook her head. "We should try to forget what happened between us."

Code took the ball out of her hand and hooked it onto a barren branch. "The way you forgot about me?"

She snapped her eyes up. "I never forgot you, Code."

Code pulled her into his arms, wrapping his hands around her waist, his fingers slipping into the back pockets of her jeans. He brought her even closer and felt her tremble from his touch. His gaze drifted down to her sweet, ripe mouth. "Prove it."

Two

Making love to Code Landon in Arizona hadn't been wise. He'd caught her by surprise. She'd never expected to see him at Tempest West. Her guard had been down, and she'd been caught up in emotion and lust and something more. Something that played havoc in her heart. He was harder now, wearing more armor than she ever remembered. She'd unintentionally broken his heart and she'd felt that anger in him when they'd made love. But he'd also been physically tender and giving throughout, even as she sensed an underlying ferocity in him.

The mistake had been made, and now Sarah was

powerless to deny him a kiss. She'd dreamed often of that one night spent with him, trying to discount her feelings, trying to put it aside and rationalize that she'd been starved for affection lately. But the truth was that Code Landon was an unforgettable man. Gorgeous. Passionate. Hard-edged. She'd loved the boy and those feelings had resurfaced even while knowing that he wasn't the sweet-natured, caring person he'd once been.

She had managed to destroy that part of Code Landon and now she knew getting involved with him would only cause more heartache.

Code brushed his lips over hers, his mouth strong and determined. His magnetic scent screamed *"man,"* and she fell into his kiss as if she'd been tossed over a cliff. There was no hope of retreat. The fall would surely be her undoing, yet she was defenseless to deny experiencing his passion, just once more.

Code pressed her closer, his fingers in her back pockets splaying across her backside and applying exquisite pressure. His manhood became apparent and she relished knowing she could bring him to such potency with just a kiss.

"Still taste like strawberries," he murmured, deepening the kiss. He rubbed against the juncture of her thighs.

"Oh." She sighed into his lips, and Code's sharp

intake of breath at that very moment told her how her pleasure affected him.

He stroked his tongue over her lower lip and she opened, garnering from him a masculine grunt of satisfaction. His tongue danced along the outer edge of hers before sweeping through and tasting her thoroughly. Trembling now, Sarah sighed once again in a conflicted state of arousal.

His knee separated her legs and he moved closer yet. Breath stole from her lungs and she could only think of being naked again with him, sharing intense passion and surrendering her traitorous body that seemed to follow his lead no matter how much she fought it.

He trailed kisses away from her mouth and she immediately missed the contact there, but soon she was immersed again when his lips trailed down her throat and his hands came up to push her sweater down past her shoulders. He pressed his lips onto her collarbone and then lower, until her nipples tightened with need and anticipation.

She'd given herself to him just once, and it seemed every cell, every nerve, every inch of her body marked the memory, an indelible imprint that would stay with her forever.

"You have too many clothes on," he whispered in a rasp. And in one remarkable move, he pushed her sweater down completely and unhooked her bra, his eyes hungry on the lacy cotton material before tossing it aside. Sarah arched her back restlessly, displaying her shameless desire.

Code lavished his mouth on her breasts, one then the other, wetting them. Then he blew warm breath onto her skin, making her prickle above the waist and tighten wickedly below.

"Oh, Code," she said, hardly recognizing the huskiness in her voice. She spread her fingers into his thick shock of short, dark hair and tugged, holding him to her.

He flicked his tongue over one extended peak, moistening the rosy circle again and again until heat pooled and swamped below her belly. She squirmed with endless need and when he finally lifted up to look into her eyes, had she been a Southern belle, she would have swooned from the raw sensuality she witnessed on his expression. Hot, hungry eyes, a face tightly drawn and a jaw set with determination.

"I want you tonight," he whispered with fierce resolve, then added, "on my terms."

Sarah was too far gone to know what he meant by that statement. And it had been a statement and not a request. But she didn't care. She'd thrown caution to the wind the second his lips touched hers and she'd known letting him touch her would lead to this.

Maybe it's what she'd wanted all along.

Maybe it was her way of making up for the past.

Or maybe she couldn't think beyond those mesmerizing deep blue eyes on a face she had always loved.

On my terms.

That couldn't be good.

Or could it?

"What does that mean exactly?" she whispered, distracted by his hands cupping her rear end and pulling her tight against his full arousal, her bare breasts crushing his chest.

"Just as I said. No holds barred. No regrets. No commitments."

His eyes turned from hot and hungry to cold and steely in an open dare she couldn't possibly refuse, not with his rock hard body pressed to hers. Not when *no holds barred* intrigued her more than the mysteries of the universe. As for regrets, she already had them, so what was one more? And for commitments? Sarah Mae Rose and Code Landon hadn't been destined for an inevitable future. She knew that with certainty.

"I agree to your terms," she breathed out, then roped her arms around his neck and kissed him senseless, obliterating his surprised expression.

Code took Sarah's hand and led her into the master bedroom, her scent enveloping him, the thought of making love to her again reeling his senses. Moonlight streamed in and encircled the room. He took a step inside, noting those inviting satin sheets and the large, accommodating bed where he planned to explore every inch of her. But one other thing stood out and smacked him with glaring force—a picture of Sarah with the Dallas Cowboys' quarterback Rod Hanson. His arm was around Sarah's shoulders and both smiled happily into the camera. The framed photo sat neatly on the right side of her dresser, directly next to a photo of Sarah with her mother and sisters.

Anger flared instantly and Code reminded himself not to get personally caught up with Sarah again. She'd broken him down once. This time was different. He wouldn't let romance get in his way. He wanted Sarah, but he wouldn't allow his heart to get involved. Glancing away from the photo, his gaze hit a box labeled "fan letters" sitting on the floor next to her desk. With pen and paper atop the desk, it appeared she'd been writing to a fan.

It was a brutal reminder that Sarah had chosen this life of celebrity over him. He could live with that now, but he'd never forget how she'd left him. He simmered with underlying anguish, closely controlled by sheer will.

He was with Sarah tonight and would make damn sure she'd never forget him again. When she thought of making love, *his* name, *his* face, *his* body would come to mind.

Code stopped by the bed and turned to face her, the dewy, soft look in her eyes causing him a moment of retreat. Then he blinked. "Kick off your shoes, baby."

Sarah did so, leaving her feet bare, her red toenails shining up in an iridescent glow.

Code rode his hands up her jeans until he reached the waistband. He unzipped her pants and pulled them down easily, along with her panties, his hands immediately returning to touch her bare skin. She stepped out of her jeans and Code skimmed his hand down below her waist, inch by inch. Her skin prickled and she sucked oxygen in. "Remember this, Sarah?"

He touched her innermost folds, one finger moving slowly, teasing, tempting, while he looked her in the eyes. Green irises sparkled back at him and she nodded.

She was warm all over, her innermost heat nearly killing him. He kissed her lips then, gently, then more firmly as his finger stroked her to match the pressure of his mouth.

She murmured a soft guttural sigh of pleasure and Code dropped to his knees. He cupped her from behind and replaced his finger with his tongue. He tasted her and stroked, holding her hips steady when she would gyrate, keeping her torturously still when she wanted to move with him. He stroked her again and again, and when she cried out, he released her hips, letting her move now frantically, her breaths quick, sharp gasps.

She was beautifully naked and in the throes of passion. Code had never seen anything so powerful in his life. Sarah, her head thrown back, her red-gold hair spilling down, a sensual sheen coating her perfect body, climaxing with sighs and cries, fully unabashed.

Code rose to face her, kissing her deeply, cupping her head and driving his tongue into her mouth.

"Code," she murmured, her breaths coming hard. "That was so…nice." She looked at him shyly.

"Nice?" he croaked out.

She let go a little chuckle and her smile brightened the room. "Incredible. Inspiring. Unforgettable. I, uh, didn't want your head to swell."

Code nodded then looked down. "Too late."

Sarah laughed. Her joy spilled over him and he smiled. Then he got serious. He wasn't nearly through with her. Code kicked off his shoes, reminded he was fully dressed. "Take off my clothes, Sarah."

He kissed her again lightly and she did his bidding, removing his shirt and planting kisses along his collarbone, then his chest. She circled his nipples, moistening them with her tongue.

Code groaned and pulled her up tight, whispering in her ear. "I need to be inside you."

She unzipped his trousers and he stepped out of his pants, but when he thought to toss her down onto the bed, she stilled him, placing her cool hand over his extended erection.

"Or maybe not quite yet," he added.

Her fingers slid over him. "No holds barred, remember?"

"I do. Glad you have a good memory, too," he managed as she stroked him faster, his manhood swelling with pulsating heat.

Code held her hips loosely and they shared potent kisses as her hands worked magic. When she dropped to her knees, Code looked down, placed his hands in her hair and swore aloud as her mouth brought him to the brink of completion.

He stopped her with a quelling hand and lifted her up onto the bed. Her outstretched arms beckoned him, and that was all the invitation he needed. He joined her, his body primed and ready to claim her.

"You don't play fair," he rasped out.

"Isn't it more fun that way?"

Code grinned and brought his body over hers. "Sarah, the games are just beginning." He parted her legs and thrust into her slowly, taking his time, witnessing the look of pure pleasure on her face. A little throaty moan escaped her lips and Code recognized that same sense of satisfaction that he felt being joined with her again.

After that first slow initial thrust, tension spiraled out of control. Her body accommodated his perfectly and she welcomed him with throaty vocal sounds that spurred his desire even more.

Ever since their first time in Arizona, Code had known their making love again was inevitable. The wait had been overly long, the heat too fiery, and when she arched her hips up and cried out a plea for completion, Code rose up and brought them both to an earth-shattering climax.

Sarah shuddered forcefully, her orgasm inspiring and so beautiful. She sighed quietly, then relaxed against the soft bed, murmuring, "You don't play fair either."

Code flopped onto his back, his spent body cooling down somewhat. He turned her way, and her sated expression made him smile. "I know, sweetheart, it's my best quality."

Sarah snuggled next to Code on her bed, his strong arm wrapped around her. Oddly, she felt at peace with him at the moment. He was a reminder of her youth and of the love they had shared when she'd been truly happy.

She'd done what needed doing back then. Her allegiance had gone to her family—her mother and sisters were living comfortably now. Sarah sang for a living and raised money for charity, her way of giving back, and if she truly dug deeply into her soul, maybe it was also her way of repenting for wronging Code Landon the way she had.

She'd gone on with her life and had become a success, feeling a sense of satisfaction and contentment.

Until Code had shown up in her life again.

She'd taken one look at him and her safely constructed world had come crashing down around her.

She stared at the ceiling adrift in thought about the boy she'd fallen in love with more than twelve years ago.

He'd been patient.

We'll wait until we're married, if that's what you want, Sarah.

He'd been protective.

I'll never let anyone hurt you.

He'd been sincere.

I'll always love you, no matter what.

Patient, protective, sincere. Now, Sarah feared Code was none of those things.

They'd made love during the night and his "no holds barred" demand had taken on new meaning. Code introduced her to a world of sensuality she'd never known. She'd given him her trust as he schooled her, taught her new positions and an awareness of her own body she'd never had before.

His fingers wove through her hair lightly and she

turned to find him watching her, those deep blue eyes that had singed her with heat last night now appeared unreadable.

"What time is it?" he asked.

"After seven."

"I should go."

She sighed and bit back words to the contrary. She wanted him to stay, but she wouldn't ask. The warmth and heat from last night seemed to have evaporated between them this morning. Perhaps both had misgivings about the hot night of sex they'd shared. She wouldn't press him. He'd asked for no regrets and no commitments.

Besides, she had an early appointment this morning with Robert for breakfast and then a tour of the Garden District. Sarah would lunch with the mayor of the city as the cameras rolled. Robert had orchestrated it all, but she couldn't fault him. If these local appearances throughout the city brought more awareness to her cause, then it would be worth it. Yet she didn't look forward to the jam-packed day Robert had planned for her. She wouldn't stop again until seven o'clock tonight, after another rehearsal with her band.

The last twelve hours she'd spent would prove to be much more enjoyable than the next twelve, but Sarah was a pro. She knew what she had to do and she never let anyone down.

Code rose from the bed and the sunlight streaming in circled his naked body like a spotlight. She'd touched and kissed every inch of him, yet she still marveled at the inspiring male specimen that stood before her. He smiled her way for a quick second, catching her raised brows, and searing heat warmed her cheeks. After the night they'd spent, nothing should embarrass her.

"I'll shower at my place," he said, gathering up his strewn clothes and putting them on.

Sarah watched his fluid, efficient movements and recalled how talented a lover he was. She'd never had a more satisfying night in her life.

Every bone in her body was sated, her limbs melting, her insides humming with satisfaction.

After putting on his shoes but not bothering to button his shirt all the way, he walked to the bed, and, with a gentle yank, pulled the sheets away from her.

She gasped. Naked to him in broad daylight, he stared down at her, raking her over with a powerful blue gaze. His hand came down and he stroked her between the thighs, a finger teasing the very tip of her womanhood. She flinched inside and heat flared. He caressed further up her belly, circling her navel, running his palm over her torso and then higher, sending a slight feathery touch over her breast that pebbled both nipples until finally his hand worked over her shoulder and throat to cup her face. His thumb slid over her lips and he parted them with mild pressure. He bent and kissed her lightly on the mouth.

"Goodbye, Sarah."

Sarah blinked. And blinked again. Before Code was out the door, she hinged her body up in bed, dragging the sheet over her breasts. "Cody?"

"No one calls me Cody anymore," he said, a finger hooking his sleek black jacket over his shoulder.

"I do," she said, lifting her chin.

"Yeah." He looked toward the door.

"What now?" she asked.

Code didn't pretend not to know what she meant. Instead he focused his gaze on her and shook his head. "I don't know, Sarah."

But she knew. The truth stared back at her with clarity as she looked into his eyes. *No regrets. No commitments.* That's all Code wanted.

She wouldn't let her pride take a beating. She'd agreed to his terms last night. Sarah smiled wide with a nonchalance that could earn her an Academy Award. "Well, then. Goodbye."

He nodded sharply, then he was gone.

"Okay, that's it," Sarah said to her band members, yanking her in-ear monitors out and lifting her guitar strap over her head. "I'm through for the day."

Betsy McKnight, one of her three backup singers

and the girl closest to Sarah's own age, stepped down from the riser and crossed the Harmony stage to take the guitar out of Sarah's hands. "You okay, Sarah? You're looking a little worn out today."

"I'm fine. Just a little tired, Bets."

"It's not like you to cut the rehearsal short."

She'd had a grueling day, but Sarah was used to long hours on the road. Today, she felt especially tired though and wondered if it had to do with the sexual workout she'd had with Code last night. "We've all been working too hard. We know this stuff upside down and backwards." She turned to her six band members, who were packing up the back line, efficiently stowing their gear away. "Take tomorrow off, guys. Do some sightseeing. Spend your money in town," she said, with a chuckle. "No rehearsal tomorrow. We're good to go."

Betsy eyed her with suspicion as she set the guitar in the case and handed it off to Brad, their bass guitarist. "Sarah, what's really up?"

She shrugged a shoulder. "I don't know. Sometimes it all gets to me. Sometimes I wonder what it would be like to live a normal life. You know, where I could go out and not be recognized. A house in the suburbs, kids. I may have grown up poor, but my mama always instilled in us a sense of family. We always had love in our house, even after my daddy took off and abandoned us."

"Man, I've never seen you so…melancholy. At least, not since that time…" Betsy held up on her thought and Sarah appreciated her consideration. Betsy had been the one person Sarah had trusted to confide in when newspaper tabloids had splashed a scandalous story about Sarah and a celebrated baseball player—a married man.

None of it had been true, but nonetheless, Sarah's name had been dragged through some pretty deep mud, putting a dull tarnish on her very polished reputation. Yet, she'd had record sales that year and found herself very much in demand.

Her fans had remained loyal throughout and she loved them for it, and eventually the general public had forgiven and forgotten. But Sarah cringed at thinking about that time in her life and how much stress the situation had put upon her.

Now, she felt another unease and it all had to do with Code reappearing in her life.

"I think I'm more tired than melancholy," she said to Betsy. "I need a good night's sleep to catch up. I'll be in better spirits tomorrow. It's been a long few days."

"Okay, but if you ever need to talk, remember Betsy's got a good pair of ears and a tight mouth."

Sarah chuckled. "I know you do, Bets. And I appreciate that."

Betsy's expression changed from mischievous to somber. "You are going straight to bed, right?"

"Right. Gosh, that sounds like heaven. I can't wait to crawl under my sheets and—" She stopped when she noticed Betsy's attention darting to the far end of the music hall. Sarah followed the path of her gaze.

Code Landon, dressed in dark clothes, sporting day-old stubble and a determined look stood at the double doors.

"Oh, my," Betsy whispered. "Who is that, and can I have one?"

Sarah groaned silently. The sight of him sped up her heart rate. Images flashed of Code's body crushed to hers on her silken sheets and the wondrous erotic things they'd done together. "He's my…uh, in charge of the hotel's security."

"He's your bodyguard?" Betsy rushed out in a low voice.

"Not really." But it seemed Code was taking up that role, regardless. "It's a long story."

"One you're planning on telling me, right?"

"Maybe…one day, Bets." As they approached, Code kept his deep blue eyes firmly set on Sarah. "Just do me a favor. Don't leave me alone with him, okay?"

"Are you joking?" But Sarah didn't smile at Betsy's jest and then her friend sobered. "Okay, got it."

Sarah knew she could rely on Betsy not to cave in. Sarah didn't trust herself with Code Landon. She didn't want a repeat of what had happened last night.

She should have never agreed to Code's terms. Sarah wasn't a *no commitment* kind of girl. She didn't enjoy casual flings, contrary to what the tabloids had written. She'd found out last night that she and Code weren't on the same page. The demands he'd made last night hadn't wavered in the morning as she'd hoped. He wanted hot sex with a onetime love, and she wanted…more.

She longed for something this older, bitter Code Landon couldn't give her. It saddened her heart to think so, but nothing spoke more clearly than Code's cold demeanor and rapid departure this morning.

"I need to speak with you," Code said, the second they got within hearing range.

Sarah narrowed her eyes. She wouldn't put up with Code's demands any longer. "It'll have to wait. Betsy and I have to go over our song sets."

Code looked at Betsy and put out his hand. "Code Landon."

Betsy took his hand and smiled. "Betsy McKnight."

"You have a great voice, Miss McKnight. I enjoyed your rehearsal."

Betsy flushed three shades of pink. "Thanks. It's easy sounding good behind Sarah."

He nodded and returned his attention to Sarah. "It's business, and it can't wait."

"Robert handles all my business. You'll need to speak with him."

Code's nostrils flared and his facial muscles grew tight. "This involves you, personally."

Sarah didn't know how much Code was willing to say in front of Betsy, but from the look in his eyes, she couldn't trust him to be discreet.

"It's about the Dream Foundation. I found you a big contributor."

Sarah blinked. The Dream Foundation was her weak spot. She had trouble keeping her excitement at bay when all she wanted to do was jump up and down with glee. She turned to Betsy. "We'll work on those sets another time, okay?"

Betsy eyed her, as if unsure how to proceed. "Okay?"

"It *is* okay, Bets. And thanks for a great rehearsal today. See you in a couple of days."

They embraced and she waited until Betsy left the music hall before turning her attention to Code. Thrilled to have another contributor on board, she asked, "Who is it?"

Code cocked his mouth up, his midnight-blue eyes squared on her. "Me."

Three

"This is Brock's place," Code explained to Sarah as he let her inside the penthouse apartment at the very top of Tempest New Orleans. "I'm staying here while he's gone."

Sarah entered and darted her gaze around, unmindful of the plush masculine accommodations. Code had insisted they speak privately, so for the sake of the Dream Foundation, she'd agreed to come up here with him.

Wary, unsure, with her guard up, she would have never submitted to this if he hadn't said the magical words. Sarah was a sucker for her charity, even if it meant Code Landon getting involved. Money was money and they needed much more than she could raise alone here.

"You were rude to Robert," she stated. They'd run into her manager in the hallway outside the Harmony Room and he and Code had had a subtle war of words.

"That guy needs to get a life," Code said, removing his leather jacket and tossing it onto a high-backed beige leather chair.

Sarah wrapped her arms around her denim jacket, refusing his offer to remove it in a crazy attempt at self-preservation and a reminder to keep the meeting short. She'd dressed comfortably for the rehearsal in jeans and running shoes but Code had a way of making her uncomfortable no matter what she wore.

"You told him I was having dinner with you. That's not true. I plan on hearing you out. Then I'm going to bed."

Code raised one brow provocatively, but Sarah didn't take the bait.

"We both need to eat, Sarah. Might as well do it together."

"I'm not hungry," she said politely. Her mama's well-taught manners always her companion, she added. "Thank you, but I don't want dinner tonight."

An amused smile emerged. "Okay, the lady isn't hungry. Got it. Have a seat. I'll get us both a drink."

"Make mine iced tea." She eyed the comfy sofa

but decided it safer to take a seat on one of the two chairs in the room.

Sarah wanted to keep her wits about her. She was exhausted. An alcoholic drink or two could send her over the edge and she didn't want a repeat of last night with Code. Not that the night hadn't been glorious, but she'd decided it wasn't worth the hollow feeling she'd awoken to in the morning with Code's cool and abrupt demeanor.

She needed to focus on the Dream Foundation and how much Code was willing to help. That's all that mattered.

Code fixed himself a shot of bourbon straight up and then emptied a bottle of lemon-flavored iced tea into a tall glass, tossing a few ice cubes in before bringing it over to her.

"Thanks," she said, trying to ignore the warming jolt swimming through her as he brushed his fingers over hers. "Now about the Foundation?"

Code took a seat across from her and leaned back, eyeing the rim of his drink. A second ticked by, then another. When he looked into her eyes, she nearly melted from the sincere depth of emotion she saw on his face. "I've made a lot of money over the years. More than I ever imagined. More than I'll ever need." Then he leaned forward and braced his arms on his bent knees and stared at her. "The Dream Foundation does good work. There's a real need here in New Orleans. What would you say if I offered to match the amount of money you raised this Christmas?"

Sarah held the glass to her lips ready to take a sip. She wouldn't dare now. The liquid would surely turn to drool as her mouth gaped open. Slowly, she lowered her glass and set it on the beveled glass table beside her. "Do you know how much money we're talking about here?"

Code smiled. "I know. Your concerts bring in hundreds of thousands."

"And you're willing to help *that* much?"

Calmly, Code sipped his drink again. They spoke like two people who hadn't been searing up her sheets twenty-four hours ago. It was kind of eerie in a way Sarah couldn't rightly fathom.

"I am."

Sarah studied him for a moment, puzzling out his intentions. "Why?"

"I'm community-minded."

Her brows shot up in surprise.

He laughed outright. "Okay. I haven't been in the past. But my accountants have contributed to many charities on my behalf. This time, I want to take an active part in helping out."

Sarah shook her head. "I still don't get it."

Code challenged her with a deep blue-eyed stare. "Are you refusing my help?"

"Don't be silly, Code. Even if I hated you personally, I'd still take your money. For the Foundation."

"You're that dedicated?"

"I am."

"Do you…*hate me?*"

Sarah took a deep breath and released it slowly. She whispered, "How can you ask me that after last night?"

Code flicked a deliberate look over her with so much heat that her skin prickled with awareness, yet he refused her an answer.

"I could ask the same about you, Code. Do you hate me?"

"No, I don't hate you, Sarah," he answered quietly.

Sarah sat up straighter in the chair, lifting her chin. He'd answered her question, yet he hadn't really said what she'd hoped to hear. He'd made no declaration about his feelings for her, whatsoever. She wanted…something from him. They'd made love on two separate occasions, and both times had touched her deeply. It seemed that Code wasn't a man who revealed his true emotions.

Exhausted now, she wanted to get back on track and deal with her overwrought feelings another time. They'd gotten off the real subject and that was his contribution to the Dream Foundation for Katrina victims. "So you're planning on matching my donations for all eight concerts?"

"I do have a ceiling, Sarah. One million dollars."

Sarah nearly stammered out her words. "Y-you're willing to donate…one million dollars?"

"Matching your concerts sounded like more fun, but yeah. I'll donate one million to your cause."

Sarah sank down in her seat and blew out a big breath. "I don't know what to say. The Dream Foundation will appreciate it."

Code nodded.

Filled with both elation and doubt, Sarah wasn't sure why she'd felt so befuddled except that she was overtired and not entirely immune to Code's generosity.

She stood up. "You're doing a good thing. The victims of the hurricane need as much help as they can get."

Code rose from his seat and approached her. "I've watched your interviews, Sarah. You're the perfect spokesperson for the Foundation."

Sarah blinked, balking that Code found anything about her perfect. "Th-thank you," she said, as doubt crept in again. Code could be very charming when he set his mind to it.

"We can work out the details later." Sarah turned to leave and when she twisted the knob and opened the door, Code came up behind her, stretching out a hand to shove the door closed.

"Code, what are you doing?" she asked, feeling foolish speaking toward the door.

She felt his presence surrounding her, and his rich masculine scent drifted in the air, an erotic reminder of last night. His hands circled her waist and applied pressure on her hips. His breath caressed the back of her neck and he nibbled on her throat. "I'm saying goodbye to you," he said, between tiny kisses.

He had a way of saying goodbye that made her want to stay forever. She closed her eyes and wished he'd stop, but the sensations he aroused created infinite pleasure that buttoned her lips and had her leaning back against him.

He brought his hands up just under her breasts, holding her from behind causing her immeasurable tremors of heat.

"You're in my blood, Sarah Mae Rose."

"I don't want to be," she said quietly, the truth astoundingly accurate.

"I don't want you to be either," he replied with regret.

She turned to face him and cocooned in his embrace, she searched the depths of his eyes for a sign of warmth or longing or compassion. When she found none, disappointment registered instantly. Then she was struck with a notion that caused her to lash out. Was the donation a bribe of sorts to secure her a place in his bed? "Is this the terms of your donation?"

Code stroked his thumb over her lips, outlining

her mouth and she was struck with a sharp pang of desire. "One is business and the other is pleasure. They have nothing to do with each other."

Oddly, she believed him yet she still issued him a dare. "Then let me go."

Code backed away from her and nodded. "You're an expert at walking away, Sarah. I won't stop you."

He opened the door and she exited, retaining some sense of composure as she headed for the elevator.

"Next time, you won't want to leave."

She didn't want to leave now.

Her skin prickled and she didn't dare turn around. That last remark put her on shaky ground because she knew if she saw him leaning against the doorjamb, watching her with those melt-your-heart eyes and a charming expression, she'd walk straight back into his arms.

As exhausted as she was, Sarah couldn't sleep. She tossed and turned and quietly cursed Code Landon for haunting her thoughts. Finally, she punched down her goose feather pillow, flopped onto her back and stared at the ceiling, surrendering to her bout of insomnia.

And then words flowed in her head, lyrics that wouldn't go away. Lyrics, that had somehow eluded her for months now came to her with ease. And the music, too, played in her head.

Sarah didn't have to write them down. She

wouldn't forget them. That's how she wrote. She'd sing the tunes silently and they would become a part of her, staying with her until she finished the entire song. Only then, would she reveal the song to her band, expert musicians who could put the melody to her lyrics, just the way she envisioned.

The next day, Sarah woke with a deep sense of satisfaction about the new song that still formulated in her head. She'd spent half the night working on it and now her eyes burned from lack of sleep.

She didn't function well on less than seven hours of rest—three was a killer. She rose from bed and plunged her arms into her bathrobe, then trudged to the kitchenette to make a pot of coffee. While the coffee brewed, she toasted two slices of bread and decided against butter or strawberry jam today. Her appetite lacked enthusiasm, and she knew better than to force the issue.

Toast and coffee would suffice today.

She moved slowly through the suite, taking a long leisurely shower that didn't accomplish the task of perking up her fatigued body. She dressed in soft pink sweats and slipped her feet into flip-flops with bright yellow daisies at the top.

By mid-morning, her mood hadn't brightened.

Only when the knock came at her door did she remember that she had a fitting for her new concert wardrobe. "Coming," she said and ambled to the door.

As soon as she opened the door, Robert entered with two of her designers pulling a rack of clothes and behind them, her make-up artist and hairdresser followed. "We've got some great pieces here," Robert said. He gestured for the women to take up the better part of her living room space, the clothes rack placed in front of her Christmas tree, making the routine invasion harder to swallow this morning.

"Good morning," she said to all, wishing she were back in bed, tucked in cozy and warm.

They greeted her with cheerful smiles.

Those smiles nearly did her in and she knew she couldn't face a day of being trussed up and painted. "Lori and Wendy, I'm sorry, but I need to reschedule with you."

Robert intervened, just like clockwork. "What do you mean, reschedule?"

"I'm not feeling well today. I'll try on the clothes, because time's running short in case alterations are needed, but I'm not up to trying new hair or make-up today."

"Sure thing, Sarah," Wendy said and Lori concurred.

"Now, just a minute," Robert said as the women turned to leave, their cases and equipment in hand. "We have to do this today, Sarah. Your first concert is on Friday night."

"Lori and Wendy know what they're doing. We

don't need a trial run." She shot another look their way. "I'm sorry for the inconvenience. Enjoy your day."

Robert's face twisted in restrained anger as the door closed behind them. Sarah had seen that look a hundred times over the years, and this time, she didn't care. She was too tired to put up with his tirades. "Let it go, Robert."

He sighed impatiently and waved her over to see her new outfits.

Sarah scanned the clothes with a discerning eye. She couldn't hold her annoyance at bay another second. "Every one of them has sequins and rhinestones. And this one," she said, holding up a one-piece jumpsuit, "has feathers! I thought you understood. I wanted subtle, not…this."

She turned to the designers whom she'd worked with on and off for her entire career. "It's not your fault. I know you only did what Robert told you, but I can't wear any of these. Not the way they are now. I'll look like a female Elvis wannabe. These are *not* me, Robert," she said calming her voice down. She wasn't a diva with princess tendencies. "I'm a simple Texas girl not a…a—"

"You're a star, Sarah. We need to let everyone know that. We've had this argument before. I've always steered you right."

Yes, they'd had this argument before, but this time Robert had gone overboard. Sarah would sooner wear a clown costume than these flashy clothes he'd commissioned.

"Ladies, give me a minute alone with Sarah," he said to the designers, anxiously walking them outside.

After he closed the door and returned to her, he shook his head. "What's gotten into you lately? You've never questioned my judgment before. Why now?"

"I *have* questioned your judgment, Robert. For years now, but you haven't listened. You don't hear me. And you're making me into someone I'm not. I can't sing if I don't feel honest about myself." Her frustration mounted as her patience grew thin. "I can't do this right now. I need some air."

She marched out of her suite, leaving Robert alone. She'd never walked out on him before. She'd never really stood her ground either. She'd woken up tired and grouchy, lacking patience with him this morning. She'd always left everything to him, and maybe that's where she'd gone wrong. There was no denying she owed him a great deal, but for once, Sarah felt justified in her demands. For once, she'd told Robert that his way wasn't the only way.

And it felt darn good.

Code had his security team situated in various parts of the music hall, strategically placed to keep an eye on the crowd, while he stood on the sidelines backstage. Gigantic pine wreaths decorated with big gold ornaments and neatly tied red velvet bows hung from the rafters. Poinsettia plants lined the front stage, and the inviting scent of pine filled the hall.

The house was sold out, and a tick worked in his jaw as he noted Sarah's fans filing into the Harmony Room and taking their seats. Even now, ten years later, it was a bitter pill to swallow thinking she'd given up the love they'd shared—a love he'd trusted, to run off with Robert Gillespie, an upstart young music producer, to make a name for herself on the country music circuit.

Code had seen Gillespie around the hotel, issuing orders, conducting business and arguing with the tour manager over input lists and lighting. There was no doubt that Gillespie had great influence over Sarah and her success. She had changed because of Gillespie, and Code hated him for that.

But he blamed Sarah most of all.

Code was here in New Orleans because of her and for no other reason.

"Are all your men in place?" Gillespie asked, coming to stand beside Code but looking straight out into the crowd.

"My team are where they need to be," Code said, keeping his irritation concealed.

"I hope so," Gillespie said. "Sarah doesn't need any more stress right now. She hasn't been herself lately."

"Maybe she's being pushed too hard," Code said, casting Gillespie a direct stare.

"Stay out of my business, Landon."

"I could care less about your business," Code shot back, then he caught sight of Sarah heading his way walking with Betsy McKnight and the other back up singers. He left Gillespie and approached her.

"I need to go over some last minute plans with you."

Sarah nodded and her back up singers moved on. "Anything wrong?"

"Not a thing," Code said, taking her hand and leading her away from Gillespie and the band members who were readying to take the stage. He moved quickly, until he'd come upon a secluded alcove behind backstage lighting equipment.

He hadn't spoken with her since that night in his hotel suite, but he'd had his team watching her routinely and been given reports. Tonight, she looked pretty in a soft denim skirt, a frilly white blouse and a big studded silver belt that accented her tiny waist. Her hair, the color of a deep sunset spilled down past her shoulders in curls, one sole crystal clip over her left ear keeping it in place.

"So what do you—"

"This," he said, pulling her into him and crushing his mouth to hers. Code couldn't get his fill. He stroked her lips and slanted his mouth over hers until both were nearly out of breath. Unlike the others who wanted Sarah because of her fame and fortune, Code felt just the opposite. None of that mattered to him. His desire for her had nothing to do with her celebrity.

"Wow," she said, staring into his eyes.

Code smiled and returned her stare. She was dressed for her performance tonight and shined everywhere but in her eyes. There, he noted the same weariness and fatigue he'd witnessed the other night. Something niggled at him. Something wasn't right. He knew how important raising money for the Dream Foundation was to her, but somehow that eagerness contrasted sharply with the loss of sheen in her eyes, the weariness that no amount of makeup could conceal and the slump of her shoulders.

"Sarah, are you up for this?"

"I'm ready, Code. Just a bit tired."

He'd known about her hectic schedule. Gillespie had her running in circles most days with giving interviews, doing radio shows, rehearsals and fittings.

"And confused," she added. "I haven't seen you in three days, and now you kiss me like—"

"You were busy and so was I."

Sarah stared at his mouth and then closed her eyes briefly. "Code Landon, you can't just come and go into my life like this. I'm not—"

"You're on, Sarah!" the stage manager said,

rounding the corner, nearly in a panic as her theme music played on stage.

"I've got to go," she said and Code watched her shift gears, becoming a celebrity entertainer the minute she crossed backstage lines and was greeted by thousands of adoring fans.

Winded after singing three encore songs to a standing ovation, Sarah walked off stage like a pro waving a final farewell to the audience.

Then promptly collapsed.

"Damn it! Sarah, wake up. Wake up, Sarah."

Sarah blinked her eyes open, dazed. She found herself lying horizontal on the floor encased in Code's strong arms. "What happened?" she asked, her mind clouded.

"You fainted," he said, leaning over her, "the minute you left the stage."

She remembered now. Her legs had been two strands of rubber while doing her last few songs. She'd been out of breath and a chill had swamped her. She'd maintained her composure until the very end. The second she left the stage, her body surrendered, her eyes rolled and that was the last thing she recalled.

She heard voices of concern surround her.

"Is she all right?"

It was Betsy. Then Robert.

"Let me see her," he insisted.

Code tightened his grip on her. "I'll take care of it," he said. "Back off, everyone. I've got her."

Code lifted her in his arms and searched her eyes, leaving no room to doubt his intentions. "You okay with that?"

She nodded, still woozy but feeling safe with Code.

"Landon, she's my responsibility," Robert insisted.

"This is a security matter, Gillespie. Back away." Then Code issued orders to a few members of his team who had congregated. "It's under control. You know what to do," he said and his employees filed out of the backstage area.

Code walked down the hallway behind the stage. "I'm coming with you," Gillespie said. "Sarah needs to see a doctor."

"No, I don't." Sarah protested with a shake of her head. A mistake. Her wooziness intensified. "I'm fine. Code, you can put me down now."

Code slanted her an impatient look. "Not on your life."

He continued on to the private elevator that led to their suites. Robert rattled on incessantly and Code ignored him.

"For heaven's sake, Robert. I'm fine. I didn't eat before the show. That's all it is. Thanks for your concern, but you don't need to babysit me. Good night," she said, dismissing him.

Code entered the elevator, leaving Robert standing there looking doubtful.

"The minute we reach my suite, you will put me down," she said to Code as the elevator doors closed. Sarah didn't like feeling helpless. She felt foolish being carried up to her suite by Code. She wasn't a damsel in distress. And Code certainly wasn't her knight in shining armor.

Since he was hell-bent on ignoring her, she closed her eyes and leaned back, trying to recoup her energy.

The next thing she knew, Code opened the door and walked inside still holding her in his arms. Instant warning bells rang in her head. "This isn't my suite."

"No, it's mine," he said, moving toward his bedroom. He pulled back the sheets on his massive king bed and set her down gently. "You won't get any rest in your suite, Sarah. I know you. The phone will ring off the hook. Now lay down and be quiet a minute while I call the hotel doctor."

"I don't need a doctor." Sarah immediately bounded up from the bed and the room spun wildly. She nearly swooned again. "Oh," she muttered and found herself in Code's arms again.

"Don't be stubborn, Sarah," he said softly now, gazing into her eyes. She liked the more soft-spoken, less demanding Code Landon best of all. "Lay down here for a while. I won't disturb you."

"You won't?" Sarah said automatically, realizing she sounded more disappointed than skeptical.

"No, I won't. But I expect you to eat a meal and go right to sleep."

Code flipped out his cell phone and called room service. He ordered her a light meal asking for a quick delivery.

"No doctor," she pleaded, already sinking into his sheets. "I'll be fine in just a few minutes."

Code sighed heavily then agreed. "Okay, no doctor, but you're not leaving this room until you eat and sleep. That means you're staying until morning."

Sarah wouldn't argue with Code. The comfortable mattress beckoned and she couldn't fight the exhaustion sapping her strength any longer. She drifted off, agreeing once again to Code's terms. "I'll stay until morning."

Four

Sarah rolled onto her back, the sexy scent of sandalwood filling her nostrils. She looked beside her and noted that the other half of the bed had been slept in, the pillow indented, the sheets pulled in haphazard fashion.

Glancing around the room, she saw her clothes set neatly over a chair with her boots lying beneath. Fortunately she recalled last night with clarity. Code had taken her to his suite after she'd fainted. She'd dozed on this bed, then woke to eat a late night dinner with him and had retired back in this room. Code had given her his shirt to sleep in and had left her alone.

Vaguely, she recalled him holding her during the night. Vaguely, she recalled his words of comfort as she slumbered. And even more vaguely, she remembered him rising early, leaving her at peace in his bed.

Noises from the master bath had her turning in that direction. Sounds of water rained down, and she realized Code hadn't left the suite after all. She heard him enter the shower and shut the door. She closed her eyes, imagining herself in that shower with him, heated by clouds of steam and Code's naked body. Her imagination took flight from there and she pushed erotic thoughts of soaping him from top to bottom and him doing the same to her, out of her head.

She remembered Code's terms. No holds barred. No commitments. No regrets.

"Sarah, don't be a fool," she whispered and heeded her own advice. She rose from the bed, feeling slightly refreshed from the good night's sleep she'd had and quickly unbuttoned Code's shirt. She removed it and grabbed her own clothes hoping to make a quiet, but quick exit.

She dressed and finger combed her hair. When she heard the shower door open again, she hastened her progress, picked up her boots and made her way out of the bedroom.

"No goodbyes, Sarah? I should be used to that by now."

Sarah stopped in her tracks, caught red-handed. She felt a little guilty for trying to sneak out on Code. He'd been cordial and concerned last night and had taken good care of her.

She turned around and her heart stuck in her throat when she came face to face with Code, his short black hair wet and slicked back, his gaze fastened on her. Water dripped on his bare muscled chest and thick forearms bunched when he folded his arms across his chest. He wore a white towel that dipped below his navel, wreaking havoc with her imagination.

"I thought I'd better go, Code," she managed, darting another glance over his chest. "It's getting late."

"So you thought you'd just sneak out of the suite?"

"I...um," she fumbled, then raised her chin, refusing to let Code intimidate her. "Well, yes. You did enough for me last night."

His lips curved in a sinful smile, his voice deep and ominous. "On the contrary, Sarah. I didn't do nearly what I wanted to do."

Sarah swallowed. Code always made her doubt her decisions. She wanted to stay, when she knew darn well she *had* to leave.

"Come here," he said, his midnight blue eyes coaxing her.

She fought her desire, her pride in jeopardy. "No."

"Afraid of me?"

"Maybe, a little," she admitted, raising her chin a notch higher.

"Because you know that we're damn good together."

Yes. Yes. Yes.

"And it's the last thing you want." Code burned her with the truth.

She couldn't respond. She let go a weary sigh. "You did something nice for me last night. I appreciate it, Code. Can't we let it go at that?"

He shot her an amused look. "Nice? You think I was being nice to you when I carried you back here, fed you and tucked you in?"

Puzzled, Sarah nodded with hesitation.

"I'm not a nice guy, Sarah. I did that for Brock. This hotel is sold out because of you. You're a no-show at the concert, and the hotel suffers. Your well-being means big bucks, so let's not pretend different, okay?"

Deeply stung, Sarah held back tears. No one could have changed so much in ten years. The old Cody wouldn't have ever deliberately hurt her this way, and she wasn't sure this new Code Landon was as cruel as he let on. "You're angry that I picked up my boots and tried to walk out on you this morning. You're angry because I don't want you on your terms, so let's not *pretend* different, okay?"

Code grinned and his whole stance relaxed. "Oh, baby. You want me, on *any* terms, and that's what's got you so rattled."

Before she could issue a heated reply, he turned and walked back into the bedroom, giving her a view of his broad back and his perfect towel-draped butt.

Sarah signed autographs for fans at the obligatory meet-and-greet prior to Saturday night's show. She performed to another sold out crowd, but the exuberance she normally felt while performing wasn't there. She faked it, mostly, and hoped her fans and critics alike couldn't tell that mentally and physically she was exhausted.

Not that she hadn't rested during the day. After leaving Code's suite this morning, she'd gone back to her own room, tried to put him out of her mind and slept for part of the day. She didn't return phone messages and had put Robert off when he'd come to check up on her. She'd taken all of her meals alone in her suite.

Now, again alone in her suite, she removed her outfit, a one-piece jumpsuit that shimmered in gold tones but thankfully sported no feathers or rhinestones. She hung up the garment in her walk-in closet and put on her most comfortable pair of heavy red cotton pajamas, slipped on matching red and white slippers and sat down in the parlor of her suite to watch the lights twinkle on her Christmas tree.

She still hadn't finished decorating it—she had three boxes of ornaments to go. With a sad smile, she remembered putting those ornaments up with Code beside her the other night. They'd had a good time working alongside each other with a sense of peace. Those were only a few happy moments in time, but Sarah treasured them. She always would, because regardless of the past or what the future might hold, Code Landon would always hold a special place in her heart.

Sarah leaned back against the plump sofa cushions. The twinkling tree lights blurred as tears swelled in her eyes. She longed for a good old-fashioned Christmas. Back in Barker in her younger days, there hadn't been a lot of money, but she recalled her mother and sisters gathering around the tree to sing carols, their humble home scented by warm sugar cookies baking in the oven.

She'd planned on going home for the holidays this season, but this opportunity to help the Dream Foundation had presented itself, and Sarah had given up her own desires to raise money for the charity.

Now, she had the chance to change lives. She had an opportunity through her fame and celebrity to make someone else's Christmas wishes come true. She took pride in giving one hundred percent of her concert take to the less fortunate and felt it was worth the personal sacrifice. Robert had called in the numbers. Her two concerts so far had netted over two hundred thousand dollars. Coupled with Code's generous offer to match the amount, she'd nearly earned half a million dollars this weekend alone for Katrina victims.

"Not half bad, Sarah Mae," she whispered in the lonely room.

Sarah went to bed and fell asleep immediately. When she woke in the morning and glanced at the clock, she did a double take.

It was nearly noon!

She rose slowly, still stunned that she'd slept the entire morning away. She showered, trying to shake off the feeling of fatigue and dressed in a pair of jeans and a black turtleneck sweater. She put her hair up in a clip at the top of her head, unconcerned that tendrils fell haphazardly down her back. "What's wrong with you, Sarah?"

And as if answering her question, her stomach growled at the same time her phone rang.

She picked up the phone instantly, warding off the shrill sound that seemed to irritate her lately. "Hi, Sarah. It's me, Bets. I've got two muffaletta sandwiches waiting to be devoured. Can I come up?"

Sarah loved New Orleans's signature sandwich, made with to-die-for olive paste on melt-in-your-mouth bread, something her band had introduced her to the last time they'd played in Louisiana. "I'd love to see you, Bets. Come on up."

Sarah knew Betsy used the sandwiches as an excuse to check on her well-being and she appreciated her concern and friendship. Her stomach growled again and Sarah silently thanked Betsy for her good timing.

"You're a lifesaver," she said minutes later, letting Betsy inside the suite. "I owe you for reading my mind. I'm starving."

"I aim to please," Betsy said, walking past her and setting a white carton down on the black granite countertop in the fully functional kitchenette. "I brought us a ton of grub."

"It won't go to waste," Sarah replied as she dug out two plates and filled glasses of iced tea. "Table or living room?" she asked Betsy.

"Living room. I want to look at your tree."

Sarah smiled and they took their meals into the front room. She knew she'd feel more energized once she ate something.

Betsy sat facing the tree glittering with lights that Sarah kept on all day and night. "Got a pretty big one this time. You must be missing home something awful."

Sarah shrugged. "My mama's spending the holidays with Aunt Edwina, but she promised she'd come to one

She wanted him.

On any terms.

That's why she'd been avoiding him lately, ducking out of sight the minute she spotted him. Code had gotten to her and that fact scared her senseless.

Hell, he didn't want a repeat of their youth either. He'd never want that. He'd told her she was in his blood and that was no lie. This time, he'd be the one to walk out on her, when the time was right.

Code had left her alone, needing a break himself. He'd spent time working at the plantation house, hiring carpenters to make repairs while he, too, engaged in some tasks. The small-town boy hadn't been completely purged from him—he liked getting his hands dirty. Working on the house was a needed distraction. He enjoyed putting hammer to nail and rebuilding something of value.

Stage lights dimmed to golden hues and Sarah sat down on the third step of the riser, singing a soft ballad he recognized as her latest country hit.

Before Code could blink his eyes, a young man rushed up on stage heading for Sarah, knocking down a poinsettia plant to get to her. Startled, Sarah rose up with fright in her eyes as the frenzied fan called out, "I love you, Sarah Rose!"

She stumbled and fell backwards, catching her with her hands, the man nearly upon her.

of the shows here before Christmas. I'll see my sisters for a short time after their midterms."

"They like school? Could never figure that."

Sarah smiled and lifted the sandwich to her mouth. Betsy's whole life was music. She'd dropped out of high school to sing backup with local rockers, but Robert had found her and seasoned her to sing country. She really was a country girl at heart, much like Sarah.

"Mmm. So good," she muttered, enjoying the first bite. Then she faced her friend. "My sisters *love* college life. They love the freedom, and being out of Barker and having independence."

"Still," Betsy said, shaking her head. "All those books and exams. I didn't care much for school."

Sarah lifted the sandwich to her mouth again, but before she could take the next bite, her stomach tightened with cramps. She waited for the sensation to pass, holding her breath. But her stomach only cramped with more pain. She set the sandwich down and closed her eyes.

"Sarah?" Betsy's voice held concern.

"I, uh," Sarah couldn't get the words out. Nausea hit her hard and she ran to the bathroom and hung her head over the toilet, making it just in time.

Ten minutes later, Betsy tucked her into bed, compassion filling her large brown eyes. "I'm worried about you, Sarah. Yesterday you fainted. Today, you emptied your stomach. You've been exhausted for days now."

"It's just a touch of the flu," Sarah said.

"It's a touch of something, but I've got a feeling it's not the flu."

"You think I'm working too hard?"

Betsy shook her head. Sarah stared at her, waiting for her next comment, because she always had one.

"My cousin Laurel had the same symptoms, honey. Nine months later little Jessica was born."

Sarah stilled, every muscle in her body immovable. Blood drained from her face and she was sure she looked like a ghost. She whispered softly, "It can't be."

"Because you haven't been with a man?" Betsy's tone was hopeful.

When Sarah hesitated to answer, Betsy nodded. "It's that gorgeous zillionaire, the one with the knock-'em-dead eyes. The one you haven't told me about entirely?"

Sarah bit her bottom lip and sighed quietly. "We were in love when we were teenagers."

Betsy nodded, encouraging her to go on.

"I left him for my career. He's never forgiven me."

"So he's the father?"

Sarah refused to believe it. There had to be a dozen other reasons for her fatigue, fainting and

nausea. "I'm not sure I'm pregnant, Be I'm not. It's just…stress and work."

"You need to see a doctor, honey. know for sure."

She couldn't deny it. "You're right, saw a doctor."

Code stood in the wings watching Sar; during her next performance. He'd watch hearsals throughout the week and it was b why she needed to rehearse—she neve mistake, never forgot the lyrics. She was the time, and her pure, natural voice could emotion in the hardest of souls.

Even his. In weaker moments. He ad talent, and that irritated him. Admitting brought joy to her fans and was loved by t only served to validate her leaving him in B; ago.

Yet, he couldn't help admire her in ot She had gumption. She'd stood up for h other day, nailing him to the wall with h tive observations.

You're angry that I picked up my boc to walk out on you this morning.

Damn straight, he'd been angry. S out on him one too many times. He w get away with it again.

His team was on the young man in seconds. Three of his best in Landon security jackets grabbed the attacker and pulled him off stage. He went kicking, screaming out his undying love for her.

Furious his team had allowed this to happen, Code rushed to Sarah's side, lifting her up. Seeing fear in her eyes and holding her quaking body, he lifted her up and carried her off stage. "Are you okay?" he asked.

She shook uncontrollably in his arms. She'd been attacked before while on stage in Nashville. She'd been distraught and shaken when that crazed fan had attacked her.

"I...don't know." Tears welled in her eyes.

"I'm getting you out of here."

Code moved quickly and wouldn't allow anyone to deter him. He called down to the garage and ordered his limo driver to meet them there.

"Get us out of town, Jimmy," he said, helping Sarah into the limo once they'd reached the lower level garage.

"Where to, Mr. Landon?"

"Willow Bend. And nobody knows about this until I decide to tell them."

"Got it."

Code wrapped his arms around Sarah and drew her closer, her slight trembling gnawing a hole in his gut.

"Close your eyes, Sarah. You're safe now."

Five

Sarah relaxed in Code's arms, her head on his chest, the solid beating of his heart a steadying comfort as they drove away from city lights. She kept her eyes closed, hearing highway sounds—rumblings of the road as the limo sped along, zipping past other cars.

She didn't have a sense of time—didn't know how long they'd been driving, but when the driver stopped the limo, Code shifted his body and the slight nudge brought her upright.

She hadn't argued with Code about taking her away. She'd been too stunned and distraught and in need of his protective arms. Now, she shook the cobwebs from her head and came out of her daze. She'd been frightened on stage just minutes ago, the incident reminiscent of the last time she'd been attacked. She'd had a difficult time dealing with it, and if it weren't for Robert's constant encouragement and support, she'd have had a hard time getting back on that horse after the fall. But with Robert's guidance and unwavering friendship she'd managed to overcome her fears and return to give her performances.

Tonight, when that fan rushed onto the stage, coming at her with wildness in his eyes, all those old memories resurfaced, and all she could think about was protecting her unborn child from the attacker.

That's when it had finally hit her.

That's why her fear had doubled from the threat.

She was pregnant.

The doctor had confirmed it just days ago, but up until tonight, Sarah had refused to believe it. She'd taken two home pregnancy tests after speaking with Dr. Linton and even then, she'd been in denial.

She had that crazed fan to thank for making her realize how precious life was and that's she'd do everything in her power to protect her unborn child.

"Where are we?" she asked, though she had a pretty good idea when she saw moonlight shining on the levee when they'd turned into a long paved driveway. She'd heard about River Road and the plantation mansions that sat along the banks of the Mississippi but had yet to visit a home here.

"Welcome to Willow Bend." Code looked straight ahead, gazing at the dimly lit house with pride. "This place survived the Great Flood of 1927, and Katrina didn't do her in either."

Sarah looked at the house more closely. Sturdy white columns supported two stories, and she recognized the impressive exterior architecture as Greek revival with a boxlike shape and wide windows spaced apart equally in orderly fashion. Bending ancient oaks graciously surrounded the property, and images flashed in her head of this home's sweeping historic past.

Code broke into her thoughts when he turned to face her. "Did he hurt you?"

She blinked then shook her head. "He never touched me. I lost my balance when I saw him coming at me." Sarah bit her lower lip and confessed, "I feel foolish now. I should have stayed and finished the show."

"You sang for two hours. No one will feel cheated. If they do, that's their problem, Sarah."

Sarah didn't agree. She had an unrelenting work ethic and didn't like disappointing her fans. She still shook inside, realizing her vulnerability. Unending fatigue and news of her pregnancy had plagued her all week. The attack on stage had been the straw that broke the camel's back. She glanced at the house. "Why did you bring me here?"

"No one knows about this place. You won't be disturbed here. If you stayed at the hotel, you'd be fodder for the tabloids and paparazzi. You'd never get out from under all the media."

"You do have a point." And Sarah wasn't up to any of it. She'd come to New Orleans with good intentions, but she wasn't up to more media attention that would sap hours of her energy. She just didn't have any to spare right now.

"I'd say thank you, but I know you're just doing this for the good of the hotel. You're protecting Brock's interest."

"Am I?" he asked, quite mysteriously.

Sarah wondered at that statement, refusing to read more into it. At this point she couldn't figure him out but she knew one important thing about him.

He was the father of her baby.

She'd better get to know the real Code Landon before she informed him of his paternity.

"Thanks, Jimmy," Code said to his chauffeur. "I'll take it from here. Remember, tell no one where we are."

Jimmy nodded and Code took her hand. "Ready?"

She wasn't entirely sure, but the strength of his hand covering hers filled her with momentary courage. "I'm ready."

Code waved off the driver's attempt to help them

from the car. Instead, he opened the door and assisted her out, making sure she was steady on her feet before closing the door. Code entwined their fingers once again as he led her up the steps. She waited on the veranda and gazed out at land that had once been sugar cane fields while Code opened the massive polished wood door.

Almost silently, the limo drove off leaving her completely alone with Code.

What are you doing here with him, Sarah?

Her nerves raw, Sarah's stomach tightened into a knot of trepidation. Panic set in. At some point she had to tell Code about the baby, but she couldn't trust him with the truth yet. She had to define their relationship, meager as it was now, in some way. Hot sex and past remorse wasn't enough of a bond to raise a child together.

Sarah didn't know what she wanted. This was all so new to her. She'd dreamed of motherhood someday, but with that dream had come all the trimmings. A man who loved her deeply, a home to call their own and a future bright with promise.

As she looked into Code's dark unreadable eyes her fears mounted. Who was he really? How could she divulge her secret and trust him to do the right thing? What kind of father would he make? Would he lash out at the child because of his unrelenting resentment of her?

Code turned on the entry hall light, and with a hand to her back ushered her inside. She took a reluctant step farther into the house and was immediately swept up by the glorious rooms to her left and right dated by antiques and wide plank floors.

She followed Code farther inside to view a large free-standing winding stairway that led to the second floor. "The front rooms are finished. The sitting room, library and dining room on this floor are being refurbished." Code showed her the rooms, many of which had large canvas tarps draped over the furniture.

"It's beautiful," she said truthfully, realizing seeing this home in full daylight would enhance her impression even more.

"Hungry?" he asked, leading her to the kitchen.

To her surprise, hunger pangs followed her into the room. "Starving, actually."

"These appliances are all in working order," he said, the kitchen the one place in the house, she presumed, that had been fully updated yet kept with the style of the rest of the home.

Code opened the refrigerator and pulled out a few large dishes. "Compliments of Chef Louis," he said with a grin.

"Who is Chef Louis?"

"Brock's secret weapon at the hotel. I had him send over some meals with Jimmy yesterday."

Code unwrapped three dishes. "Chicken and andouille gumbo, rosemary chicken or jumbo lump crab and mango cake salad. Anything sound good?"

Sarah reminded herself not to put her hand to her belly, something she'd been apt to do since she found out about the baby. Thankfully, her nausea had subsided and all three dishes sounded like heaven. She picked the safest of the three choices. "Rosemary chicken."

Code set the glass dish in the oven and turned it on. He gestured for her to take a seat. "How about a drink?"

"Mint julep would be appropriate in this house." A nervous laugh escaped and she caught Code's raised brows. "But I'll settle for a glass of water."

She sat down.

"No wine?" he asked, leaving the room. Seconds ticked by and he returned with what looked like a very expensive bottle. "I've got a damned good wine cellar just off the kitchen."

"None for me. I'm not much of a drinker, Code."

"I know," he said, setting the wine bottle down. "I remember." Code's eyes twinkled. "One beer, and you'd be all over me."

Sarah cleared her throat forcefully, blocking out the image of sipping beer in the back seat of Cody's car and crawling into his lap, deep in the throes of passion. So often they'd come close to making love, their breaths labored, their senses heightened, but they'd never succumbed to their desires.

Code sat and leaned toward her, bracing his elbows on the table. "I used to debate about offering you beer. Much as I enjoyed it, you'd leave me so damn aroused, I'd finish the six pack off and curse my bad luck falling for you with every sip."

Heat raced up her throat and a flush stole over her face. "I...I didn't know that. You never told me."

He shrugged. "You wanted to wait. And I wanted to do right by you."

"You were patient." The statement hung in the air until she finished, "and I loved you for it."

A light flickered in Code's eyes for a moment, before he inhaled sharply and turned from her.

Sarah made herself busy setting out plates and utensils Code handed her, wishing she could've taken back those words. When the food was ready, they shared a quiet meal, neither of them bothering to speak as they ate, their past looming overhead like a dark, ominous cloud.

After they finished eating, Code rose and offered her his hand. "Time for bed, Sarah."

Sarah gazed up at him, the blue in his eyes gleaming like the deep fathomless sea.

"Do I need to ply you with beer to sleep with you tonight?"

Sarah closed her eyes briefly, caught up in bittersweet nostalgia and intense emotion. She took his hand. "No."

"That's good, baby, because there's only one bed in this house, and you're sharing it with me."

Sarah gazed out the master bedroom window overlooking the Mississippi River watching twinkling stars dot the sky with bursts of light. She stood on unsteady legs, wishing she could drink a beer to bolster her nerve.

Then she scoffed at the notion.

She'd been alone with Code before. They'd made love. But now, knowing Code would play a role in her future because of the baby put her on the shakiest ground of her life.

She hugged herself around the middle letting a deeply held breath escape.

"Cold?" Code stood behind her, wrapping his arms around her waist, his breath warming her throat, his smooth voice sliding over her like soft velvet.

"I'm not sure."

"You're not sure if you're cold?" he asked with amusement.

She gave her head a slight shake. "I'm not sure I should be here…with you."

She looked over her shoulder and viewed his handsome profile. The sight of him so near made her dizzy with desire.

"You didn't complain when I carried you off that stage."

"I was scared."

"You're still scared, aren't you, Sarah? But you trusted me enough to let me bring you here. You could've stopped me."

"Would you have listened?"

"No, probably not," he admitted, his hands roaming down to the waistband of her suede form-fitting pants. He splayed his fingers wide and applied exquisite pressure to her flat stomach.

Sarah closed her eyes and thought of the tiny baby his hands warmed. In softer moments like these, she could fall deeply in love with Code again.

"I'm glad you're here with me," he said quietly. "I wanted you to see Willow Bend. One way or another, I would have brought you here."

"Because I'm in your blood?" She peered straight out the window, standing as still as the columns that supported this house, waiting for his answer.

Code moved in front of the window, blocking out starlight. He fingered a lock of hair that had crossed her forehead, gently pushing it back behind her ears. Their eyes met and Code bent his head and brushed his mouth to hers. "Yes, you're in my blood, Sarah," he whispered in the darkness, "But I won't fall in love with you."

Sarah understood why. She'd hurt him in the past,

and he'd never trust her again. She'd left Barker, Texas, for fame and fortune. Code would never see it any other way.

Now that she'd been forced to face him here in New Orleans, her heart ached for all that they'd lost. She'd never loved anyone as much as she'd loved Code Landon. He'd been her first love, and they'd adored each other. She didn't have a witty reply. She didn't feel the need to burn him the way his words had scalded her. Sadness swept through her, and she turned away from him with tears in her eyes.

Code grabbed her arm gently and she stilled. In a fluid motion, he lifted her into his arms and carried her over to the bed. Setting her down, he covered his body over hers and crushed her lips with a spellbinding kiss. She responded to him, wrapping her arms around his neck and kissed him back with unrestrained ferocity.

He was in her blood as well.

She hadn't realized it until this very moment. Even armed with the knowledge that Code would never love her again, she couldn't deny him. She couldn't deny her own desire either. Maybe she, too, needed to find a way to get him out of her head and heart forever.

Making love to him isn't the way to do that, Sarah.

Sarah shook off her niggling thoughts. She couldn't fight him any longer. Emotions took over and Sarah surrendered to them. After her fright tonight on stage, she needed his strong arms around her. She needed his body crushed to hers. She needed to feel safe with him by her side.

She wove her hands in his hair, messing up his trimmed military cut as he unbuttoned her gold silk blouse. He wasn't one to finesse, Code took what he wanted, and once he removed her blouse and bra, his hands caressed her breasts, thumbing the nipples until every nerve in her body screamed out in agonizing joy.

He watched her as she accepted his sensual touches, his eyes burning like dark embers. "I like putting that look on your face, baby."

He flicked his thumb over her again and she moaned and curled her body further under him, needing more. "I like when you put that look on my face. But I like the way it feels even more."

Code kissed her again, driving his tongue into her mouth and making contact immediately while one hand continued to caress her. A hot flush warmed her entire body.

Code stopped kissing her to gaze upon her, his eyes roaming over her leisurely. "I pictured you in this bed with me a hundred times."

Sarah's throat constricted from the sheer power of his gaze. "When you pictured me, did you have on all your clothes?"

Code let out an amused chuckle. "Smart ass."

"Am I?"

"Hell, when I pictured you here, neither one of us had a lick of clothes on. Neither one of us could move a muscle once we exhausted each other. And neither one of us wanted to be anywh—"

With a frown marring his handsome face, Code stopped short of saying neither one of them wanted to be anywhere else. But Code couldn't trust in that, much less finish the sentiment. Something powerful clicked in her heart. It was another reminder of what they'd lost and would never regain.

"Well, then, Mr. Landon, with all this picturing in your head, I'd say you need to get very busy."

"I like a demanding woman," he said, standing to full height and unbuttoning his shirt. "In bed, that is."

He stood over her with his shirt hanging from his broad shoulders and leaned toward her. "It's a shame these have to go," he said, helping her slide her feet out of her boots.

He rode his hands over her smooth suede pants. "And these."

She helped him with the side zipper and he yanked them off playfully. "Be careful with my pants."

Code looked at the pants he held in his hands and shook his head. "Do you really care?"

Sarah peered at the custom designed suede pants she'd fought Robert so hard to keep in her wardrobe and realized how ridiculous she sounded. It had been her win against Robert and not the pants that she cherished so much. She smiled. "No, I truly don't. It's just that they're one of a kind."

Code flung them. Then he gazed down at her naked form with hunger in his eyes. "You're one of a kind, Sarah."

He returned to the bed after removing his trousers and kissed her deeply, his tender words sweet to her ears. She'd become familiar with him, the musky male scent of his skin, the taste of his mouth and the powerful way he held her.

He stroked her between the thighs and she parted her legs, allowing him to slide his hand over her apex. She moved under the ministrations of his fingers, rotating her hips, her breasts swelling and her body igniting.

He readied her quickly, her juices warm and wet. As he rose over her with protection in place—protection that she no longer needed, he teased her with the tip of his potent erection. Anticipation stirred her senses wildly.

"Hang on."

His tone left no room for doubt. She took hold of his shoulders and rocked back with the power of his first thrust.

A satisfied moan escaped her throat. She clung on

to him as he plunged farther. Wracked with tremors of ecstasy, she moved her body with his.

"So damn good," he said between fiery kisses and thrusts that left her speechless.

It seemed the whole of his concentration was bent on pleasuring her and he got an A+ for effort.

"Code," she called out, when his hard erection brought her senses to the brink. Her body heated and electricity surged like a lightning bolt. Her orgasm pulsed through her system with force and her hips gyrated to accommodate that demand. Her powerful release met with Code's and they rose up together to a fevered pitch, then slowly lowered down, their rapid breaths mingling, stealing the remaining oxygen in the room.

Spent now, she rested back on the bed, her emotions in turmoil, but her body singing an opera. Code was a marvelous lover. She'd only been with three other men in her life. Three men she'd cared about and not the dozen famous athletes and actors the tabloids had associated her with, but no one would ever come close to Code's lovemaking.

They had intense sexual chemistry. It's a mystery how she'd been able to put him off all those years ago. Thinking back on it now, she didn't know how she'd kept from jumping his bones on those backseat dates.

Code rolled away from her and lay on his back

staring up at the ceiling, his expression unreadable again.

"Cody," she began softly, wanting so badly to tell him everything she felt in her heart. Maybe tell him about the baby she carried.

"Don't say anything, Sarah." He rose slowly from the bed and faced her again. "Just don't say anything."

He strode to his antique armoire, opened a drawer and pulled out a shirt. He handed it to her and then picked up his pants and headed for the door.

"Where are you going?" she asked rising up, confused and in a bit in a panic.

"I need a drink. Get some rest. I'll be back later."

And Code walked out of the room, leaving her sexually satisfied and completely baffled.

Code raked a hand through his hair and poured three fingers of bourbon in a tumbler. He paced the parlor floor sipping from his drink, the liquor sliding down his throat with ease.

Memories flooded his senses of Sarah Rose, the high school freshman so pretty and fresh-faced and sweet approaching him in Barker Hall, handing him a flyer for the dance on Saturday night.

"You have to come," she'd said. "We're raising funds to send care packages to our soldiers for Christmas."

Touched by her generosity and enthusiasm, Cody accepted the flyer and asked a few questions, just to have Sarah talk to him awhile longer. "My father was in the military," he'd said.

Sarah's smile grew wide and her pretty green eyes brightened. "Then you have to come."

Code had rocked back on his heels pretending nonchalance. He'd been taken by Sarah from the moment she'd approached him and knew then and there he'd wanted to know her better. "Well…I don't know."

"Please." She had pleaded with genuine concern.

"I don't dance."

"I'll teach you," she'd offered and Code made a date with the auburn-haired girl without hesitation.

That had been thirteen years ago. They'd fallen in love almost immediately and had been youthfully, naively happy. Code had admired Sarah's generosity. She'd always tried helping others, even when her family's situation had been dire. They'd been beyond poor, her mother trying to raise three girls on her own.

Code hadn't forgotten the desolation and gut-ripping pain that seared his system when Sarah's mother, Lenora Rose walked up to him one summer day. "She's gone. She asked me to give you this."

Shock stole over him. He thought he'd heard wrong and questioned Lenora, who had tears in her eyes.

He barely remembered reading Sarah's letter. He'd trembled uncontrollably.

So much had happened since then and neither one of them could have predicted the outcome of their lives.

Code finished his bourbon and glanced at his watch. It would be earlier in the evening in Hawaii. He sat on a wide velvet-tufted chair, picked up the phone and punched in Brock's number.

"Hey," he said once Brock answered. "I figured you've heard about what happened tonight."

"Yeah, man. I did. Got a call from my manager. What the hell happened?"

"Some jerk rushed up on the stage. We apprehended him before he got to Sarah, and he's being dealt with."

"How's Sarah doing?"

"Scared, but okay. He didn't touch her physically, but it was enough to bring back some old memories of being attacked on stage. I plan on getting to the bottom of it. My team never lets anything like this happen. Something's up, and there's going to be hell to pay."

"I take it you've got Sarah," Brock stated without doubt.

"I do."

"Where?"

"Willow Bend. I'll keep her out of the limelight for a day or two. She needs the rest and quiet."

Brock laughed, his mirth coming through clearly.

"You're telling me she'll get that being alone with you?"

Code wasn't a kiss and tell kind of guy. "Yeah, something like that."

"Oh, man. I suppose you told her you took her there for her own good."

"No. I told her the truth. I'm protecting your interest in the hotel. She's the reason you're sold out for the holidays."

Brock kept silent for a few seconds. "That's just plain wrong, Code."

"It's the truth."

"No, the truth's staring you in the face, and you're too damn prideful to see it." Then Brock sighed and added, "Listen, I owe you for taking care of her. I don't want anyone getting hurt at my hotel, much less a sweet person like Sarah. I'm not holding her to her contract. If she can't perform again—"

"She wants to. In fact, she said wild horses wouldn't stand in her way."

"She's doing this for charity," Brock said, "and I admire her gumption. Maybe you should cut her some slack."

"Me? You want me to cut *her* some slack?" Code wasn't offended. He and Brock spoke openly about many things, but Brock seemed to have the situation backwards. It was Sarah who had treated him unfairly. "I'm only protecting yo—"

"*Her.* You're protecting her because you care about her more than you're willing to admit."

Code balked at the notion. He wouldn't fall in love with Sarah again. He couldn't. Sarah cared about her career and regardless of her charity work, she still loved being a celebrity.

"Cody?"

Code turned to find Sarah standing on the bottom step of the winding staircase, wearing only his shirt, her coppery hair a mass of wild curls, her pale face framed by faint light.

Something tightened in his gut—the same something that had him getting up and leaving Sarah alone in his bed tonight. She looked like she belonged here at Willow Bend, in his bed and in his home. She looked…*perfect.*

Code couldn't take his eyes off her. "I'll call you tomorrow," he said to Brock and hung up, then rose from the parlor chair. "Sarah?"

"I, um," she began, but couldn't seem to get the words out. She nibbled on her bottom lip.

Code called himself every kind of fool. He'd brought her here, made love to her after she'd had a frightening night, then had left her alone to sleep in a strange bed in an unfamiliar house.

She stared at his bare chest, her eyes filled with longing. Code walked over to her and met her piercing gaze. "I'm here."

She swallowed and nodded.

He took her hand, entwining their fingers and walked her back upstairs to his bedroom, where she promptly fell asleep in his arms.

Six

Telling Code about the baby she carried had been on the tip of her tongue for the past two days. In that time, she'd spent every waking moment with him at Willow Bend. Her days were filled with taking long walks along his property, cooking meals together and sitting by the levee before the winter chill would send them back inside the house.

She watched Code work on projects around the house and often he'd look up at her with deep hunger in his eyes, promising another night of earth-shattering passion. Yet, Code kept an emotional distance from her. She felt his restraint in his every touch, the tone of his voice, the hard edge surrounding him that she couldn't seem to breech.

Sarah had to go back to the hotel today. She couldn't put off her duties any longer. Her sudden disappearance had only spurred speculation from the media. In the past, she'd been slapped with scandals that had marred her good name. She needed to make an appearance before the speculation got out of control. Robert had been especially demanding of her when she'd finally telephoned him. She'd defied his command to come back which only angered him more.

Sarah flipped the griddle cakes and watched them break into little bubbles as they sizzled. She couldn't help smiling as she made breakfast for Code. He'd always loved griddle cakes. Part of her couldn't believe that she stood here, half-naked in Code's shirt, cooking for him, while the other part of her couldn't believe how much being at Willow Bend with him had come to feel like home.

"Don't wish it," Sarah mumbled to herself.

He still hasn't let down his guard.

Sarah didn't know if she could trust him with the truth about the baby. She was cautiously optimistic, but hadn't yet found the right moment to let him know he was going to be a father.

At one time in their lives, starting a family had been their ultimate dream.

"Something smells good," he said and she turned to find him standing in the kitchen threshold, watching her. Sarah stilled, and her heart raced. It seemed every time he entered a room, the *thump, thump, thumping* beat out a rapid rhythm she couldn't control.

Fresh from his morning shower, he was sexier than any man she'd ever known. Jeans hugged his slim hips and a shirt hung unbuttoned from his broad shoulders exposing a gloriously tanned and muscled chest. His hair dried in disarray, and he hadn't seen a razor in days. Tiny love marks all over her body served as evidence.

She turned toward her task, picking up a plate and sliding the spatula under one round griddlecake. "They're almost ready. Want to eat out in the garden?"

Sarah loved the burgeoning gardens outside. A newly restored lattice gazebo sat amid flourishing shrubs and flowers along a brick path ten yards from the back entrance of the house.

Code came up behind her to wrap his arms around her waist. "Not if it means you putting on more clothes."

She filled the plate and set it down near the oven, giggling when Code nuzzled her throat. "Code, I'm trying to fix breakfast."

She was the ultimate cliché, making breakfast dressed only in his shirt, barefoot and pregnant.

"And you're doing a bang-up job, baby." He fondled her breast.

Playfully, she shoved him away. "Go, pour the coffee or something."

They'd had a two-day break from reality. Sarah rationalized it as trying to acquaint herself with the man he had become. Yet, they'd never spoken of the future, living only in the moment.

Code set the cups of coffee down on the table refusing to let her put on her clothes to eat outside. She laughed, bringing a tall stack of griddle cakes to the table. "You're the most insatiable man I've ever met."

He grinned and tugged on her hand until she landed into his lap. She anticipated his kiss, but a loud booming knock from the front door startled her. "Who could that—"

Code lifted her off his lap and rose before she could finish her thought. "Wait here. I'll get rid of whoever it is."

He headed for the front door, buttoning his shirt as he strode out of the kitchen.

Seconds later, Sarah heard volatile voices raised in argument. She couldn't make out the words, recognizing only Code's deep tone, the other voice being female.

Female?

Sarah headed toward the front of the house and

PLAY THE
Lucky Key Game

Do You Have the LUCKY KEY?

and you can get

FREE BOOKS
and FREE GIFTS!

Scratch the gold areas with a coin. Then check below to see the books and gifts you can get!

YES!

I have scratched off the gold areas. Please send me the **2 FREE BOOKS** and **2 FREE GIFTS**, worth about **$10**, for which I qualify. I understand I am under no obligation to purchase any books, as explained on the back of this card.

326 SDL EVMH   **225 SDL EVQT**

FIRST NAME	LAST NAME

ADDRESS

APT.#	CITY

STATE / PROV.   ZIP / POSTAL CODE

www.eHarlequin.com

2 free books plus 2 free gifts   1 free book

2 free books   Try Again!

Offer limited to one per household and not valid to current subscribers of Silhouette Desire® books.
Your Privacy – Silhouette Books is committed to protecting your privacy. Our Privacy Policy is available online at www.eHarlequin.com or upon request from the Silhouette Reader Service. From time to time we make our lists of customers available to reputable third parties who may have a product or service of interest to you. If you would prefer for us not to share your name and address, please check here. ☐

DETACH AND MAIL CARD TODAY!

(S-D-11/08)

© 2008 HARLEQUIN ENTERPRISES LIMITED. ® and ™ are trademarks owned and used by the trademark owner and/or its licensee.

The Silhouette Reader Service — Here's how it works:

Accepting your 2 free books and 2 free mystery gifts places you under no obligation to buy anything. You may keep the books and gifts and return the shipping statement marked "cancel". If you do not cancel, about a month later we'll send you 6 additional books and bill you just $4.05 each in the U.S. or $4.74 each in Canada. That is a savings of at least 15% off the cover price. It's quite a bargain! Shipping and handling is just 25¢ per book, along with any applicable taxes.* You may cancel at any time, but if you choose to continue, every month we'll send you 6 more books, which you may either purchase at the discount price or return to us and cancel your subscription.

*Terms and prices subject to change without notice. Sales tax applicable in N.Y. Canadian residents will be charged applicable provincial taxes and GST. Offer not valid in Quebec. All orders subject to approval. Credit or debit balances in a customer's account(s) may be offset by any other outstanding balance owed by or to the customer. Please allow 4 to 6 weeks for delivery. Offer available while quantities last.

stopped up short, seeing Code in the vestibule nose to nose with a gorgeous raven-haired woman. From her quick glance out the window she noticed a long, black limousine in the driveway.

"You're wrong, Maria. I *don't* want you here. We're over."

The woman's dark Spanish eyes contrasted against the sleek lines of her white pantsuit and faux fur jacket, and burned with determination. "We were in love. Can you throw that away so easily?"

"It was a mistake. I don't know how many ways I can say it."

She put her palms flat on Code's chest, caressing him. "Let me change your mind, *mi corazon.*"

Sarah's gut clenched and jealousy caused a sharp gasp to slip out.

Both heads turned in her direction. The woman's gaze fell on her with stunned surprise when she recognized Sarah. Most people who knew music did, some of her country songs crossing over to the pop culture. Sarah couldn't say she hadn't been in the forefront of entertainment news on many occasions.

The woman further scrutinized her noting Sarah's state of undress. Her eyes darkened with anger and pain. In her haste, Sarah had forgotten she wore only Code's shirt. Uncomfortable now, she shifted her feet from side to side.

Sarah glanced at Code who had the composure to introduce them. "Sarah Rose, this is Maria Marquez."

"His fiancée." Maria lifted a haughty chin.

"*Ex*-fiancée," Code clarified.

Maria cast him an injured look and her voice softened with anguish. "Is *she* the reason you do not call me back?"

Code swept his gaze to Sarah then to the broken-hearted woman. "You tell me, Maria. I'm here with her and not you."

Maria flinched at his tone as she seemingly made the same assumption based on Code's claim. Another quick glance at Sarah, and Maria appeared convinced.

"No, it's not like that," Sarah blurted, furious at Code for his insinuation.

Code shot Sarah a warning glare then turned back to Maria. "You need to go home, Maria. We are through."

True tears spilled from Maria's eyes. "I see," she said softly, unable to hide her hurt expression. "I was a fool."

Sarah watched the scene, sympathizing with the woman who obviously was still in love with Code. She couldn't believe Code's harsh tone or the brutal way he'd dismissed her.

Maria turned on her heels quickly ready to leave, then spun around to heed Sarah a warning. "Do not trust him with your heart. He is cold…like stone."

Maria exited with a regal gait, her head held high, but her wobbly shoulders as she retreated gave away her sobbing. They watched as her chauffeur opened the door, and Maria got into the limousine without so much as a glance back.

Once the car turned onto River Road, Code turned to her, his lips tight. "Sorry you had to see that, but it was good timing that you were here. Maria—"

"*Good timing?* That she saw you with another woman? That you rubbed salt into her wounds? That you probably broke her heart…again!"

"Getting engaged was a huge mistake. I've told her that a dozen times."

"You were cold to her, Code."

Like stone.

"She needed to let go."

"You hurt her."

"I've tried letting her down easy. She's spoiled and headstrong and used to getting her way. She needed a reality check."

A chilling shiver ran down Sarah's spine. She buttoned her lips as trepidation steamed just below the surface. Seeing how Code handled his ex-fiancée convinced her she couldn't tell him about the baby. She couldn't possibly know how he'd react. She couldn't fathom what sort of demands he would make. When care and tenderness were called for, Code had exhibited callus disregard. Unfortunately, she'd witnessed that trait in him too many times to ignore.

She couldn't trust him with her precious secret.

"I need to go back to the hotel today." Sarah stared at Code, daring him to defy her. "It's time."

To her surprise, he only nodded. "I'll have Jimmy pick you up in an hour."

And just like that, the two days of bliss they'd shared was obliterated.

Twinkling Christmas tree lights and shiny ornaments greeted her when she arrived back at her hotel suite, bringing a bittersweet smile to her face. Sarah would've liked to spend this Christmas with her baby's father, to have a quiet dinner in front of the tree and to contemplate the next yuletide holiday, which would include rattles and toys and all sorts of baby gear.

Now Sarah knew that wasn't possible.

She took a long, hot bath, soaking away tension and stress. She'd tried to ignore Robert's text messages and calls, but the man was persistent, so she returned his call and listened to his tirade about her leaving for two days.

"Do you know how hard it was for me? I get one phone call from you in two days. You take off with that, that...James Bond wannabe, ignoring my messages—"

"I called you as soon as I could," she defended.

"And asked for your patience. You knew I was okay. I'm entitled to some time off."

"You mean away from me?"

"No, I don't mean that at all. Don't make this personal, Robert."

"It is personal! You're my responsibility."

She was his meal ticket.

Sarah squeezed her eyes shut at that niggling thought. Her successes made Robert a very wealthy man, but he'd earned it, she told herself. He'd worked hard, though she didn't always agree with his methods. Sarah had been young when she'd been introduced to the music industry and she'd let Robert call all the shots. It's what he did best. But now, Sarah had some doubts as to his role in her life.

"Maybe it's time I took more responsibility for myself, Robert. Maybe I—"

"Sarah, don't talk crazy," he interrupted, his voice laced with something she hadn't heard before—alarm. Robert felt uncharacteristically threatened. "We're a team, me and you. Maybe you do need to rest. I'll come by later, and we'll have dinner together. We really need to talk."

Sarah wouldn't argue. She was tired and distraught over Code. "Fine. I'll see you later."

"I'll come for you at seven."

She hung up the phone and climbed into bed, the bleakness of the cool, cloudy day matching her mood. Grateful for the reprieve, she knew she couldn't escape seeing her manager tonight.

In the beginning, he'd pursued her like a man on a mission. But as a young girl, Sarah's feelings for Robert didn't amount to more than friendship and respect. With eight years separating their ages, at times she'd thought of him as an older brother and maybe a father figure, though she'd never admit that to him for fear of injuring his male ego. Thankfully, he'd given up his pursuit of her years ago and had concentrated his efforts on work.

Sarah's mind drifted to the new life she carried inside and the reality of her situation struck her anew. "I love this baby already," she whispered, surprised at the surge of protectiveness she felt.

She had to do what was right for her child.

If someone could just tell her what that was, she'd be eternally grateful.

Sarah managed to get two hours of sleep despite her worries, certain the demands of her pregnancy tired her out more than usual.

She rose and dressed for dinner in a light gray cashmere dress that hugged her body, lending comfort with soft warmth. She draped a leather belt along her waist and donned her favorite pair of black leather boots, leaving her hair down in curls.

When the knock came at seven o'clock, she opened the door, and Robert walked inside briskly, his face animated, his eyes alight and determined. "I've got great news, Sarah. I couldn't wait to tell you about it. Are you rested and in a better frame of mind?"

Sarah narrowed her gaze. She wasn't in a better frame of mind and something warned her that she wouldn't like Robert's good news. "For what? What kind of news?"

"A country-wide tour. While you were gone these past few days, not only did I fend off the press about your sudden disappearance, but I tentatively booked you for a four-month tour, starting in the spring. We'll have lots of work to do, putting it all together, but it's going to be—"

"What?" Her nerves jangling, her voice broke with irritation. Surely, he wasn't serious? "What are you talking about?"

Robert glanced at his watch impatiently. "We're going to be late for dinner. Let's get going, and I'll tell you all about it."

Sarah stood by the threshold of the front door, completely shell-shocked. "No, Robert. I'm not going anywhere with you until I make you understand. I never agreed to tour the country this spring. You know I've been leaning toward slowing down. I want—"

"This is just what you need," he said, speaking over her, not really listening at all. "Trust me, Sarah."

"Robert, I don't want to go on tour this spring. I've told you I didn't want to tour *at all* next year."

Robert's face fell and a deep frown pulled at the corner of his mouth. "You'll change your mind. Let's discuss this over dinner."

"No," Sarah said, folding her arms across her stomach, clear now about her priorities. "I won't change my mind. I plan on taking time off after Christmas. I'd *always* planned on that, and you know it."

"Sarah, this is good for your career. You're on top now, and it's my job to keep you there. A spring tour is just the thing to—"

"I can't go!" Frustrated at Robert's persistence, her voice rose to a falsetto pitch. Maybe if she weren't pregnant she would have given in, because that's what Sarah had always done in the past. She'd let her manager make her decisions. But this time, she put her foot down, literally and figuratively.

Robert caught her foot-stomp and arched a curious brow. "You *can't* go? What does that mean?"

"I'm pregnant," she blurted and immediately wished she'd held her tongue.

She hadn't wanted to divulge her secret to him so soon. She'd wanted time to adjust to the idea. To tell the baby's father first before she had to deal with her business manager.

Robert's eyes went wide. "You're *pregnant?*"

The words repeated back to her sounded strange. A lump formed in her throat. She swallowed and nodded. "Yes."

"Who?" he asked, then shook his head and began pacing, contemplating. "Never mind. I know it's Landon. Doesn't matter."

"Now do you see why I don't want to tour?" Sarah put her hand to her belly. "I'm having a baby," she said softly.

Robert eyed her for a moment, scratched his head then a spark entered his eyes. "You can still tour. We'll get married. Hell, we're always together anyway. I'll raise the child as my own and we'll tell the press we've been in love all along. It'll not only save your image. but you'll get tons of—"

"Robert! I can't believe what you're suggesting. I tell you I'm having a baby and all you can think of is how to explain away my pregnancy to the press? You're worried about my image? What about what I'm *feeling?* What about the *baby* I'm carrying? And the baby's father? He has a right to know. You'd actually secretly raise another man's child as your own just to…just to—"

And then it hit her like a baseball bat to the head.

The realization made her dizzy. Her head spun. She looked him squarely in the eyes and saw Robert Gillespie for the man that he was.

Dozens of images popped into her head of his manipulations and the unyielding way he'd controlled her from the moment they'd met. It was all clear now and Sarah blamed no one but herself for allowing him so much control.

"Sarah, come on. It was a dumb move getting pregnant, and I'm offering you a way out. You know you can't do this alone and—"

"She won't have to." Code entered her suite, his jaw tight, his expression chilling. He shot Robert a hard look of disdain.

Sarah cringed. None of this was happening the way she'd imagined. Code must have overheard most of the conversation from outside the halfway closed door. And Code's cold blue eyes weren't solely aimed at Robert. He glanced at her. "It's my baby."

It was a statement of fact. He knew. She nodded anyway as confirmation. Code glanced at her belly for a moment, his blue eyes softening, then flicked her a look of disgust.

She released the breath she'd been holding when he returned his attention to Robert. "You're a first-class bastard, Gillespie."

"This is between Sarah and me."

"Like hell it is," Code said, his voice laced with venom. "She's carrying my child."

"She didn't tell you about it. You had to overhear it from the hallway."

Code cursed and walked toward Robert with deliberate steps. Sarah stepped between the two men. "Stop this. It's time I took control of my life."

She turned to Robert. "You're fired. We're through, Robert. I want you out of my suite right now."

"Sarah," Robert said impatiently, as if she were a whining child. "You don't mean that."

"I do. Please leave." Sarah stepped away from the two men, her nerves raw, her body trembling.

"I'm not leaving. You're upset right now. We need to discuss this. Alone."

"No, Robert," she said shaking her head. "We won't discuss this again. I'm sorry, but I won't change my mind."

"You ungrateful—"

Code grabbed Robert's arm. "Shut up. I'm giving you a choice, you can walk out with me civilly right now, or we can do this another way. And believe me, I'm sorely hoping you get stubborn."

Robert's nostrils spread as he inhaled a deep breath and looked at her. Sarah glanced away. This was the hardest thing she'd ever done in her life, aside from walking away from Cody all those years ago.

But her decision was made. And it had been a long time coming.

Out of the corner of her eyes, she saw Robert yank his arm free and walk out, his head held high.

Code was right beside him but before he exited the suite, he turned to her. "Don't move a muscle, Sarah. I'll be back. I'm not through with you yet."

Seven

Code found her standing with her shoulders slumped by the Christmas tree, staring at the twinkling lights. Darkness had descended on New Orleans and the tree lights reflected against the sliding glass door, bringing color into an otherwise dismal room.

Anger, betrayal, elation and curiosity warred within his gut and he clenched his fists, seeing Sarah looking forlorn by that tree. The sparkling lights seemed to mock her with cheerful colors, while Sarah's mood appeared anything but joyful.

"He's gone," Code announced. "For now. But I don't trust him."

Sarah didn't turn his way. She nodded and continued to stare at the Christmas tree.

Now that he'd dealt with Gillespie, it was time to deal with Sarah. "How long have you known?"

"Awhile," she said, with no further explanation. She was pregnant with his child, and she hadn't bothered to tell him that he was going to be a father. They'd spent days and nights at Willow Bend together. It wasn't as if she hadn't had ample opportunity. Damn her for not telling him. For not giving him any sign that she could be trusted.

"Arizona?" he asked.

She nodded.

They'd made love while at Tempest West in Arizona. At the time, Code thought that he could move on from that erotic encounter, but it hadn't been enough. His plan had backfired. He hadn't purged Sarah from his system at all. He'd come to New Orleans in direct pursuit of her, vowing to leave her once he felt he could get on with his life.

Now, they'd be tied together by their baby.

The realization that Sarah Rose carried his child warmed his heart. He'd thought back on their youth, when they'd fantasize about making babies and raising a family. He'd dreamed about that for years, up until the day that Sarah left him in Barker, Texas.

His dream died along with his heart that day.

Nothing had changed.

And nothing would change, other than he wouldn't let Sarah run off with his child.

"We're getting married. The child will have my name. My protection. Afterward, you and I will divorce. I'll want custody rights."

Sarah turned to him, her face crumbling. Tears fell from her eyes. "You hate me that much?"

"I don't hate you, Sarah," he said, softening his tone. "I never have."

"I'd planned on telling you about the baby. I just needed…some time."

Code walked farther into the room. He stood between her and the Christmas tree. "You've always got an excuse, don't you? But if I hadn't walked in on you and Gillespie, chances are I might never have known about my child. You would have left New Orleans and hidden it from me."

Sarah wiped tears from her cheeks. She whispered so low that he barely heard her. "How can you think that of me?"

"You told *him,* the man you fired. You trusted him more than me."

"You didn't give me any reason to trust you."

Code released a sigh. "Doesn't matter now. All that matters is that you marry me and have a healthy pregnancy."

Sarah blinked away another bout of tears, nodding.

"I agree," she said. "Nothing is more important to me than my baby."

Code looked down at Sarah's flat belly, imagining the child growing inside, hardly believing it. "I'll make the arrangements."

Sarah turned away from him then, facing the window and the bleak shadowy night. "I want to keep the marriage secret, just while I'm here in New Orleans."

Code's gut clenched. What was she up to now? "Why?"

"For my sanity and the health of the baby. With what happened the last time I was on stage, I don't think I can take more press."

She put a protective hand to her stomach. Code found he wanted to do the same, to make it all seem real. To cover his hand over the baby and relay the love he'd already begun to feel. But he remained stoic and listened to her admission.

"The media would never leave me alone, and I'm not up for any of that right now. I need to think of the baby first, and besides, I don't want any attention directed away from the real reason I'm here, to raise money for charity."

That made sense. Code wasn't too keen on being involved in the media circus surrounding Sarah if news of her sudden marriage got out. They'd delve into both their pasts and probably concoct stories about their lives in Barker, Texas that were more false than true. "Is the baby healthy?"

Sarah's lips curled up in a cautious smile. "Yes, very healthy."

"And you?"

"Aside from the fact that I just fired my business manager of ten years? And that I've been offered a marriage proposal that no woman would ever dream about, I'm fine, Code." She stepped back and cast him a defiant glare. "Just fine."

"Good." He knew his tactics hadn't been charming, but he couldn't chance Sarah's refusal. She had to marry him. He wouldn't have it any other way. "I'm glad we're in agreement."

"I'm only marrying you for the baby's sake. Just so we're clear."

"Oh, we're clear, Sarah. And just so you're clear, I'm going to have a say in what you do from now on. That child you're carrying is a Landon and I'm responsible for his safety."

Sarah let go a deep weary sigh before steadying her voice with resolve. "Don't push me, Code. I'm perfectly capable of taking care of myself and the baby. I don't need a watch dog."

Code's honed patience faded fast. "Well, what the hell do you need?"

Tears filled her eyes again. She shook her head and said quietly, "Nothing…from you."

Code let go a vile curse and at the risk of upsetting her more, he walked toward the front door. He'd have to tread lightly. Sarah looked worn out and fatigued. Keeping Sarah and his child healthy had to be his first concern. "I'll make the wedding plans and let you know when and where."

She turned away from him before any more tears fell. Sarah wore her heart on her sleeve and that was one thing Code had always loved about her. She never could keep her sensitive emotions hidden.

Now, he'd have a sleepless night haunted by the sight of her silent misery.

"Yes, Mama, I know it's happening very suddenly," Sarah said into the phone. She rested on her bed, looking up at the ceiling, praying that she wouldn't be struck down from her deception. Sarah would rather think of them more as half-truths and lies of omission than what they really were.

Out and out lies.

Yes, she was marrying Code, but the marriage was temporary and would end in divorce. She would make her excuses later on—the marriage didn't work out—they'd tried and failed—they weren't meant for each other after all.

Sarah had friends whose marriages had lasted less than six months. It was a sad state of affairs to be certain, but this way she'd protect her family from the truth.

"I want you to come for my wedding," she said to her mother. "It won't be anything fancy, just a simple ceremony. Code and I are keeping it a secret for a time."

"Sweetie pie, I wouldn't miss my baby's wedding for nothing. I don't care about fancy doings, just as long as my baby girl is happy. I always knew in my heart that you and Cody belonged together."

"Yes, Mama." Sarah cringed, despising her deception. But her mother had always blamed herself for her and Code's breakup. She'd thought that Sarah would have led a happier life had she married Code Landon all those years ago. Sarah rationalized her lies, telling herself that this way, her mama would see that she and Code were not suited at all and come to realize that Sarah had chosen the correct life path by leaving Texas when she had.

"After all these years, you two found each other again. I've prayed for this, Sarah honey. Every day, I prayed that my baby would find happiness."

"Oh, Mama. I've been…happy."

There was silence on the other end of the phone and then the sound of her mother's broken voice came through, "We all know what you did, Sarah. You sacrificed because your mama couldn't provide for you and your sisters."

"No, Mama, that's not true!" Sarah refused to let her mother take any blame for Sarah's decision to leave Barker. "Daddy left you with three children to raise. You did your best and we love you for it."

"Sarah…I let you leave…I shouldn't have ever done it."

"No, Mama, I wanted to go."

She'd had to go. Her mother's rheumatoid arthritis had jeopardized her job and her secretarial skills had been diminishing as her illness worsened. Lenora's pride matched her determination, and she'd kept her secret from her employers, but Sarah had known her mother wouldn't have lasted much longer on the job.

She'd come home at night in agonizing pain.

"It's just like you said, God gave me a voice to do something good."

"Oh, sweetie pie," her mama began as her voice broke and Sarah could tell she held back tears, "you did something good, honey. You provided for your family, when I…couldn't."

Sarah ached for her mother's pain and guilt. They'd had this conversation several times over the course of her lifetime, and Sarah never found words enough to convince her mother that she hadn't been to blame for any of it.

"I'm glad you're coming out for the wedding, Mama. I'm going to try to get Selia and Suzette to come, too, if they can get away from their classes."

"Those girls will be comin'. They wouldn't miss you marrying Cody. My, I remember how much they looked up to that boy. Little as they were, they had big ole crushes on him."

"I remember." Sarah hadn't thought about it in years, but Cody had charmed all the Rose women. Her younger sisters had admired him because he was older and handsome but mainly because he'd never treated them like children.

When the conversation ended, Sarah closed her eyes and rested. She couldn't believe that her wedding ceremony was only a few days away and would take place just hours before her Saturday night performance.

At least she'd have her mother and sisters there. Still, all of this happened so quickly, and her decision to tell half-truths to her family was made hastily. But she believed protecting them and saving her mother from more blame was worth the price of her own guilt. Sarah couldn't get married without her family present despite the fact that the marriage was a lie, and she felt like a fraud.

Sarah would do everything in her power to honor her commitment as wife and mother. At least *her* vows wouldn't be spoken in vain.

Sarah spoke her vows on Saturday afternoon on the steps of the gazebo in the backyard garden at

Willow Bend, dressed in an ivory taffeta gown. Code stood beside her wearing a crisp black Italian suit like a second skin, his tone steady as he spoke promises he fully intended to break. Brock Tyler attended as his best man, and since Sarah needed the support all three Rose women acted as attendants during the ceremony, her mother sitting in her wheelchair and her two sisters beside her, smiling and eyeing her with joy and Code with youthful fascination.

Cool winds blew and clouds shadowed the sky, yet the grounds looked lovely, and the mansion's glorious splendor and history belied the deceit that was her wedding. Sarah shivered, her sleeves ruffling in the wind as she tried to hear the minister's words before the breeze carried them off.

When the minister nodded encouraging her to speak her vows, Sarah ignored the tightening in her stomach. She spoke softly and on cue, "I do."

Code peered at her with softness for a moment, before it was his turn to respond to the minister's question. Code answered, "I do."

The clergyman offered up a wedding blessing and pronounced them husband and wife.

Sarah shook, her entire body trembling, catching Code's immediate attention. In the breadth of a second, he removed his jacket, wrapped it around her shoulders and requested that everyone save their congratulations until they went into the warm house, where an early dinner would be served.

Code led her toward the house, whispering so that only she could hear. "You look beautiful today, Sarah."

Her body warmed considerably until he added, "At one time in my life all I wanted was to marry you and raise a family."

"You make it sound like I never wanted the same thing. You know we both wanted a future together."

He slanted her a cynical look. "Doubtful, sweetheart." When they reached the back entrance to the house, Code stopped to wrap his arms around her waist, and she was certain it appeared like a loving embrace to all onlookers. "Pretend you're happy, Sarah," he said, his lips near her ear. "Put a smile on your face. I'm lying to your family because you insisted, so make a good show of it or your cover will be blown."

Then he cupped her chin and kissed her long and deep before ushering her into the house.

Minutes later, Brock came up and gave her a peck on the cheek. "Congratulations, Mrs. Landon. You make a beautiful bride."

Sarah smiled. "Thanks, Brock."

She wished she felt beautiful on the inside. Right now, the well-meaning lies she'd told her family reared their ugly head like a monster from the deep. Guilt and regret churned in her stomach. Not only had she lied to the people dearest to her, but she would have to keep this secret hidden from the rest of the world. She was married and pregnant with a child she had always wanted—Code's child—and she couldn't tell a soul.

"It's okay, honey. I know."

She snapped her gaze to Brock's intelligent dark eyes and whispered with alarm, "He told you?"

Brock scratched the back of his head and sighed. "He didn't have to. I figured most of it out on my own. When I backed Code into a corner, he told me the rest of it."

Sarah lowered her voice. "My family doesn't know a thing. Not that they'd be upset about the baby, but what comes after…would surely send my mother over the edge. She'd start blaming herself all over again if she knew how much Code really resented me."

Brock took her hand in his. "Hang in there, Sarah. Code's stubborn, but he's a good man."

She shook her head and glimpsed Code charming her sisters and mother in the dining area. Sarah hadn't seen her mother smile so much in ten years. "I wish I could believe that." Then she turned to Brock. "Please keep what you know to yourself."

"Don't worry," he returned, giving her hand a gentle squeeze. "You can trust me. C'mon, let's walk over there, and you can reintroduce me to your gorgeous sisters."

"Sure thing, as long as you know they're off limits."

Brock pumped his fist to his chest. "You're wounding me, Sarah."

"Somehow I think you'll survive."

He grinned playfully, "Always."

"Thanks for coming to the wedding," Sarah said, all joking aside. "I know you have your hands full with the hotel in Maui."

"Hey, I don't mind flying halfway across the world to see two people I care about get married. It was an honor."

"Says the confirmed bachelor."

"Yeah, well, my older brother Evan got married, and my younger brother Trent is engaged, and my best friend Code is secretly wed. Guess I'm the last hold out. Someone has to stand up for all the bachelors of the world."

Code would be a bachelor again before long, too, and that thought brought myriad emotions, but she pasted on a pretty smile as she approached her family.

She was the happy bride, after all.

While Sarah and the other guests enjoyed Chef Louis's white fondant decorated lemon cake, Code wheeled Lenora Rose into the parlor. When he'd first laid eyes on her today he'd been shocked to see her sitting in the wheelchair. Another secret Sarah had kept from him. He remembered her as a kind, prideful woman who'd had a tough life, worn down from fatigue, trying hard to keep her three daughters one step above poverty.

Now, she appeared more…rested. And happy. But Code couldn't miss the grotesque arch of her fingers or the slump of her body. Every so often, she'd stifle a wince of pain, and he knew that though she'd had the utmost in health care, she still suffered from her chronic ailment.

"My, this room has history," she said, darting her gaze around at the antebellum antiques. "The paintings are lovely," she said, her eyes filled with wonder. "Thank you for the tour."

"You're welcome," he said. Upon her request, he'd taken her through each of the lower rooms, explaining his plans for renovations. "The house is shaping up."

"You've done well for yourself, Cody. I couldn't be more proud of you."

Humbled by her comment, Code was at a loss for words.

"Will you sit down with me for a spell?" There was a breech in her voice as tears entered her eyes.

Code positioned the wheelchair so that he faced her when he took a seat. She reached her hand out and he took it, marveling at the frailty in those disfigured fingers. "I can't tell you how happy I am that you and Sarah found your way back to each other. It does my heart good, Cody."

She smiled and twin tears fell down her cheeks.

"Yes, ma'am," he said, taking out a hanky and gently wiping at the moisture. He was a sucker for tears and Lenora's kind words were enough to do him in. "Those are happy tears, right?" he asked softly.

Code's insides quaked with regret. He damned Sarah for persuading him go to along with this deception. Her mother had expectations of a fruitful, loving marriage.

She didn't answer. Instead she put her head down for a moment, then cast him a sincere look and spoke quietly. "I've always liked you, Cody. You were a good boy, and my Sarah loved you to distraction. I know her leaving hurt you bad. It hurt her, too, though she pretended that leaving you and Texas behind was what she wanted. I know she did it for me. And the girls."

She pulled her hand free of his. "Look at these hands." She lifted them slightly and Code glanced at them because she'd asked. "All I had was secretarial skills. It paid the bills, Cody. I had three girls to raise. I didn't know how to do anything else. Sarah was old enough to realize that I was about to lose my job. I couldn't do the work anymore."

Code inhaled sharply and nodded in understanding.

"It was a bittersweet blessing that Robert Gillespie spotted her singing at the county fair. It meant that we had a chance." Her voice wobbled and she struggled to keep it steady. "My girls wanted to go to college and I could barely keep food on the table."

"I understand," Code said, trying to ease her burden but stiffening at the mention of Gillespie's name.

Sarah had written him just one letter after she'd left town, promising to write more, promising once her career got going, they'd be together again. Like an idiot he'd waited for her. That was eighteen months of his life he'd never regain. While he might forgive Sarah for leaving initially, she had no excuse for not keeping her promises to him.

Memories flashed of him trekking to Memphis for one of her shows. He'd watched her from the back rows. He'd longed for her and planned on confronting her, but he'd never gotten that far. Once he'd managed to get backstage, he'd found her being escorted out of her dressing room with Rod Hanson, the cocky football star, laughing and giving him her full attention.

Then and there, he vowed that Sarah would never make a fool of him again.

Lenora's voice cut into those painful memories.

"The day I came to you with Sarah's letter." She closed her eyes and waited, as if mustering the courage. "Was the worst day of my life."

"Lenora, you don't have to—"

"Please, Cody. Let me explain. It broke my heart to see the pain on your face. You were stunned and angry, but mostly you were heartbroken."

"I loved Sarah very much."

"And I didn't give you a chance, did I? Do you remember what I said to you that day?"

Code nodded, but he wouldn't repeat it. He remembered every word in that conversation like his worst nightmare.

"I said, 'Don't go after her. She doesn't want you to.' I crushed your last hope, and it killed me. Oh God, Cody. I hope you'll forgive me."

"Mama?" Sarah interrupted, sweeping into the room with one hand holding up her gown.

She was gorgeous, the way he'd always pictured his bride to look, dressed in a white flowing gown, her pretty auburn hair restrained by the diamond headpiece he'd given her just before the ceremony. She'd done the whole wedding thing to perfection for her mother and sisters' sakes.

Yet she was his bride today and he allowed himself to look at her with a measure of pride.

"We're just having a chat," her mother said, patting Code's hand and giving him a warning look not to reveal their conversation. "Cody's been telling me about the house."

Code assured her with a quick wink, then gazed at Sarah. She darted glances at both of them with narrowed eyes. "You've been gone awhile."

Code stood then and approached her, changing the subject. "I should get you back to the hotel. You'll need time to rest before the show tonight. I'll have Jimmy bring up the limo."

Lenora managed her wheelchair around to face them, a smile lifting her lips. "I'm looking forward to the show, sweetie pie. It's been months since I've seen you perform. The girls can stay, too."

Sarah smiled warmly at her mother. "I'm so glad you're all here, Mama. It'll be nice knowing you're in the audience tonight."

"You're doing a good thing, Sarah—raising money for the less fortunate."

"Code's helping, too. He's matching the ticket sales with his own money."

Lenora's eyes sparkled with admiration when she peered at him. "You married a generous man, Sarah."

Code hadn't blushed since high school, but he felt heat rising up his collar. And he damned his new bride for that, too.

Eight

After the show, Sarah and Code walked her mother back to her room, Code pushing the wheelchair with Selia and Suzette just steps behind.

Sarah missed her younger sisters, but she knew they were happy going to college. Both of them earned good grades, Selia the more studious and Suzette the social butterfly. Sarah was proud of them and witnessing their progress and the futures they might one day have made all her heartache worth it.

"It was a great show, Sarah," Suzette said. "I never thought you needed Robert as much as he wanted you to believe. I never liked him." She wrinkled her nose. "I'm glad you got rid of him."

"Quiet, Suz." Selia warned.

"Oh, Selly, just admit it. You never liked him either."

"Smart girls, your sisters." Code gave them a thumbs-up.

"We're not discussing Robert on your sister's wedding day," Lenora said. "Hush now, both you girls."

When they reached their room, Code bent down to give Lenora a kiss. "Sweet dreams, mother-in-law."

Lenora's light hazel eyes beamed joy. "You're the closest thing I have to a son now, Cody."

"Thank you," Code said with a sweet smile, but Sarah noticed his shoulders stiffen.

He turned to kiss Selia and Suzette. "It was great seeing you two again. Good night."

Her sisters embraced Code and offered congratulations again. Sarah hugged her sisters then kissed her mother. "Want me to come inside for a while?"

"On your wedding night? Sweetie pie, I taught you better than that. You go on. You have yourself a fine husband now. Go, enjoy yourselves."

Code took hold of her arm. "Come on, Sarah. You heard your mama. It's our wedding night."

Sarah bent to give her mother one last kiss. "Okay, I'll see you in the morning. Good night."

Sarah waited until the girls helped her mother inside their suite and closed the door. Code stood waiting for her, his jaw tight, his lips pursed.

Hardly a happy groom.

"What?" she asked, her patience on a short fuse.

Code kept his voice low as they walked down the hall to his penthouse suite. "I don't like lying to your mother."

"Well, I just love it," she said, her anger boiling over.

"She doesn't deserve getting her hopes up about our marriage."

"Well, aren't you one to talk. *Mr. 'Sweet dreams, mother-in-law'.*"

"I'm only going along with this because you said it was necessary to keep from hurting her more."

"That's right," she said, entering Code's suite when he opened the door. "I explained all that."

"Hurting her is inevitable, and it's a damn sight better telling her now than living a lie and deceiving her for months and months."

"Code, you promised."

He glared at her, his eyes bitter with regret. He'd married her today, and remorse was written all over his expression. Her pride injured, her ego stung, there was no turning back now.

She'd dressed like a princess today, hoping for an ounce of joy on her wedding day. Didn't a girl deserve at least that much? Apparently, Code didn't think so.

He never failed to remind her how she'd screwed

up their lives. Sarah had hoped her charity work would somehow compensate for the hurt she'd caused.

Sudden exhaustion struck her, and everything seemed to shut down at once. Her body sagged, her eyes burned with fatigue and her heart ached so badly, she just wanted to go to bed and stay there for days.

"I'm turning in, Code. It's been a long day."

She turned to leave and Code gripped her arm, stopping her before she opened the front door. "Where do you think you're going?"

"To my…suite."

Code pinned her with blue-eyed intensity and shook his head. "You're my wife now, babe. You're sleeping here."

"But my things are all in my—"

"I'll send someone to get what you need tomorrow morning."

"Code," she said, putting up a stopping hand. "This isn't going to work."

"Your family will get awfully suspicious if they find you sleeping in your own suite."

"Are you saying that when they leave tomorrow I can go back to my suite?"

He shook his head again. "No. I told you, I'm going to have a say in your life, and I meant it. There's three bedrooms in this suite. Take your pick.

I'll make sure you have everything you need by morning. No one will disturb you here, not even me."

Sarah opened her mouth to spit out a witty reply, but then thought better of it and clamped her mouth closed. She couldn't believe she'd married Code Landon today. It all seemed surreal and darn it, she was too darn tired to argue anymore. "Fine."

Code nodded. "Good."

They stared at each other.

Seconds ticked by.

Then he approached her, his face steeped with regret. She couldn't think beyond those midnight blue eyes staring straight at her, pinning her down so she couldn't move. He reached out to touch her face, his fingers skimming her skin. Her heart warmed, her nerves tingled. He bent his head and crushed his lips to her in an earthmoving kiss that obliterated all the sins of the past. While his mouth covered hers and their tongues entwined, she forgot all else but the familiar heady taste of him. His musky scent turned her on. His hard body pressing hers sent a satisfying jolt through her system. Her sensitive breasts tingled. A pulse of awareness below her waist caused a desperate ache. When Code broke off the kiss, looking aroused and sexier than a man had a right to look, Sarah's breath caught. She wanted more.

"Good night, Sarah." He released her and backed away leaving her with a niggling thought. She was his wife now and the irony was sadly almost laughable.

From now on she'd be sleeping alone.

Sarah woke up grumpy. She didn't sleep well and now as her stomach growled, she knew she'd have to get out of bed to eat breakfast. She couldn't forego any meals. She was determined not to let down another soul in her life, most especially her new baby.

She laid a hand on her belly. "Are you warm and cozy in there? I hope so. I'm going to take the best care of you." Then a disgruntled thought entered her mind. "Even though your daddy doesn't trust me to provide for you, I *will* make sure you have everything you'll ever need."

Except a loving home.

Tears stung her eyes. Her child will never have a father and mother raising her in the same household. The baby will never know the joy of true family. Sarah had always longed for that. Being the oldest, she had slight recollections of her mother and father holding her, laughing with joy, their sweet, carefree smiles embedded into her mind. Those happy times faded fast. Her father left the family right after the twins were born, though he really hadn't been around much before that.

Now, her sweet innocent child would be a victim of a broken home.

Sarah showered and dressed quickly, her stomach growling again reminding her she needed nourishment. She walked out of the bedroom beckoned by the aroma of fresh coffee and a mingling of other delicious breakfast smells, eggs, toast, melons and other fruity scents.

She headed for the dining table just off the kitchen, but a bright light caught her eye and she turned toward the parlor and a silent stunned gasp escaped.

Her Christmas tree, adorned by her treasured ornaments sat in front of the window, the tiny colorful lights reflecting off the panes of glass. "Code," she whispered.

And she turned to find him standing behind her. Tears spilled down her cheeks at the thoughtful gesture. He'd had the tree moved here from her suite. He'd known what that Christmas tree meant to her.

She gazed at him, unable to hide her gratitude. Her hormones were working overtime. She'd never cried so much in her life as she had since Code reentered it.

"Don't cry, Sarah," he said softly. "It's just another simple wedding gift."

She glanced down at the magnificent emerald wedding ring he'd placed on her finger yesterday, to match her eyes, he'd said. A ring she would have to hide in her jewelry case from now on. He'd also gifted her with the diamond headpiece to put in her hair. He'd been generous, and she wondered if he considered it an investment, something he'd want back in the divorce settlement.

Ashamed of the unkind thought, she banished it from her mind. "Thank you."

At times, glimpses of the sweet boy she'd once loved came through. *That* Code Landon she'd never stopped loving.

"Are you hungry?" he asked.

"Starved. I'm eating for two and the baby doesn't let me forget it," she answered. "My appetite has come back, full force."

"Breakfast is ready. It was delivered a few minutes ago, so it's still hot." Code's gaze drifted down to her lacy chartreuse nightie. "How did you sleep?"

Not well. Not after that kiss that left her wanting. "Great. How about you?"

"I never have trouble sleeping."

Sarah refrained from grimacing. Code could be so doggone infuriating at times. Late last night when she couldn't sleep, she'd gotten up and popped her head inside the parlor. She'd found him pouring himself a drink from the bar.

"Now what?" she asked, completely baffled by Code's shifts in moods from kind and generous to cold and calculating. Who was this man she married?

"Now? You do what you normally do. Starting with eating breakfast."

She followed him into the dining area where an array of food crowded the table. "All this?"

"I'm eating, too. And I have a healthy appetite."

He poured her a glass of fresh squeezed orange juice. "Sit down. Want some decaf coffee?"

"No thanks. I'm good."

Sarah piled eggs, toast and fresh fruit onto her plate and dug in. She ate two helpings, including three thin link sausages and drank several glasses of orange juice. Shoving the plate away, she leaned back and couldn't stifle a bout of giggles.

"What?" Code asked, his face breaking into a smile.

"I'm not even full. Imagine that. I could eat a third helping without blinking an eye. I never eat this much."

"You've never been pregnant before."

Her smile faded. "No." She placed her hand on her belly, a gesture that was becoming second nature with her now. "Lots of things will change, I suppose."

Code sipped from a mug of coffee then leaned forward, bracing his arms on the table. "For me, too. I just want you to know I'm not unhappy about the baby. I plan on being a good father."

Sarah looked down and fidgeted with her napkin,

keeping another round of tears at bay. "I know you'll be a good father, Code."

"The baby will want for nothing."

"Except," she blurted, then restrained from saying more.

"Except?" Code's tone demanded a response. "What can't I provide for my child?"

Sarah shook her head. "Nothing, Code."

"You have something on your mind, Sarah. Just say it."

Sarah buttoned her lips. How could she admit to him she wished the marriage were real? How could she tell him if only he would trust her again she'd prove to him that they could make it work for the baby's sake?

How could she reveal that really deep down in her heart she would never love a man the way she'd once loved him. That she'd be willing to give the marriage a genuine try to give their child a sense of family, a father and mother who loved each other.

True, Sarah had her mother and sisters and she'd loved them dearly, but their family hadn't been complete. She'd never felt like part of real family with a father who would drop her off at school in the mornings, plopping a good-luck-on-your-test kiss on her cheek, like the other girls and a mother who had time to help her with homework after school. Sarah knew her mother did the very best she could for her children. But she'd always dreamed of providing a better kind of life for her own child.

Perhaps stubborn pride and ingrained precaution worked against her. She couldn't relay her heartfelt emotions to Code right now.

"Sarah?"

She rose from the table. "I've got a doctor's appointment tomorrow afternoon. He's arranged to see me as his last patient. Would you like to take me?"

Code's impatient glare while waiting for her to answer him, disappeared. He cocked her half a smile. "Yeah, I wouldn't miss it."

She nodded with relief. "We'll have to be discreet. I don't want to draw any attention."

"Right," he said, standing up to meet her gaze, his face now hard as steel. "We wouldn't want anyone to know country's darling Sarah Rose got knocked up and had a shotgun wedding."

Sarah winced. Any mention of her celebrity made Code hot under the collar. Tears welled in her eyes again, not from his harsh words, but from the realization that Code would never accept her for who she was.

She turned on her heels, unwilling to let Code see her cry again. She couldn't seem to control the tears, a drawback to pregnancy.

"Sarah, wait." Code said. He reached for her and drew her into his arms. Comforting her, he held her close.

She sobbed quietly as he held and soothed her, stroking her hair and giving her a taste of the tenderness she craved from him.

Sarah had never felt so lost. So hopeless.

And she prayed it was just her pregnancy mood talking. Because if it wasn't, then her dream of having a real family life, was just that…a dream.

The doctor's appointment went as planned, Code driving Sarah to the office in an ordinary black SUV. He'd waited until the absolute last minute to usher Sarah out of the car. The receptionist greeted them immediately, showing them to the room where Sarah undressed in a small alcove and came out wearing a blue-checkered gown.

She appeared a little self-conscious, casting him a shy smile as she sat atop the examining table. "Not very fashionable, is it?"

Code cocked her half a smile. Sarah always looked great, whether wearing jeans and a T-shirt or a stunning sequined gown. Today, she'd worn a tan suede skirt and a cream colored blouse that made her skin glow and her eyes look like fresh new grass.

Doctor Linton came in a moment later and introduced himself.

"Code Landon, Sarah's husband," he said. It dawned on him that was the first time he'd actually said those words aloud. They sounded strange to his ears. He was Sarah's husband, and she didn't want anyone to know about him.

"But, for obvious reasons, no one is to know she's married or that she's with child. I hope you'll comply with our wishes."

"Certainly," the doctor stated. "It goes no further than this room."

Sarah's celebrity ensured many people's understanding of the situation. Though Code did Sarah's bidding, it irked him that she'd wanted to keep the baby and their marriage a secret. Code recognized his irritation for what it was—his ego bruising, and he didn't like it. Not one bit. Yet as the examination progressed and the doctor explained to both of them what to expect in the upcoming months, reality hit him with striking force.

They, he and Sarah, would bring a child into this world. Hearing the beating of the baby's heart brought it all home.

For those few unfettered minutes, Code forgot about the terms of their marriage arrangement. He weighed in on every word of the doctor's instructions. He listened intently to Sarah's questions. He asked questions of his own. He fell into the role of husband and father-to-be and gauged a cautious look at the awe and love in Sarah's eyes as the doctor spoke of their baby.

"So the baby is due by summer?" she asked.

"Yes, at your next appointment we'll do a sonogram to give us a more accurate accounting of time. In the meantime, continue with your regular activities. Just be more aware of your body signals. Get the rest you need."

"I plan to," she said, bobbing her head up and down. "I don't have much planned after this series of Christmas concerts. The baby is the most important thing in my life."

Code noted the sincere look on her face. Did he believe her? He wasn't sure what to believe, other than she carried a new life inside and both of their lives would change forever.

Code walked Sarah back to the car after the appointment and glanced at his watch. It was late in the afternoon, and he wasn't ready to take her back to the hotel yet, where each one would go into their separate rooms for the evening.

"Are you tired?" he asked.

"Not at all. Hearing the baby's heartbeat perked me up." She set her hand on her stomach in a protective manner. "I can't believe it, but it's really happening, Code."

He inhaled sharply and nodded. "Pretty daunting, isn't it?"

She peered into his eyes and a genuine look of joy crossed her features. "Yes, in a good way."

He kept his expression steady, but inside, he

warmed up considerably. He had no doubt Sarah would love the child she carried, but would she give the baby higher priority than her career?

"I know this out-of-the-way place in the Quarter. Mellow jazz and good eats."

"If you're inviting me, I'm accepting."

"I'm inviting."

"Then I'd love to."

Code made a phone call then drove from the heart of the city into the French Quarter, just a few miles from Tempest New Orleans. He parked the car and came around to get Sarah.

"Just a minute," she said, dipping into a big black leather handbag and coming up with a curly brown wig. "For emergencies," she said with a big grin, tucking her hair under the short wig and plopping wide-rimmed glasses onto her face. "My red hair is a dead giveaway."

Code frowned for a second then once the transformation was in place, he chuckled. Even with his security background, he doubted he'd recognize her from a distance. "Gotta admire your ingenuity."

"Comes from necessity. Hazards of the job."

"Are you saying you don't like the attention?"

"Code," she said, batting her eyelashes, adjusting to the glasses. "I'm a singer. I love to perform. Unfortunately, that means being scrutinized in my private life. And no, I've never liked that."

He took that comment at face value and helped her out of the car. They walked behind a restaurant, followed an old brick path and entered Smooth Tones, a small crowded club sandwiched between the restaurant and a voodoo magic shop. "This *is* out of the way," she said. Gentle jazz sounds rose above the hum of conversations from the packed tables and dance floor and flowed softly. "I love it."

"Let's have a seat," he said, taking her arm.

Sarah darted her gaze around. "Where? Doesn't seem to be any available."

When an empty corner table magically appeared, Code gestured to the trumpet player his thanks. "My table."

"*Your* table?"

Code offered Sarah a seat and then he sat down next to her. "Do you own this place?" Sarah asked quizzically.

"Not really. Let's just say, the place had some trouble with robberies a while back. My company stepped in, took care of the problem, but not before they'd accrued a lot of debt. The place was ready to close down, and I saw it as a good investment. I loaned them the money they needed to get back on their feet."

"And they pay you back with dinners and hard-to-get corner tables."

"Something like that. They have the best gumbo in the city. "

Sarah smiled. "I feel like a different person, being here in this place, completely out of the limelight."

Code had to smile his agreement. "You *look* like a different person." No matter what Sarah Rose did to disguise herself, she still was beautiful. Those frumpy glasses and that curly wig only made her appear more appealing to him. She went from wholesome gorgeous to cute and adorable within a matter of seconds.

There was something so irresistible about her tonight. Maybe it was that damn disguise and her resourcefulness, or the closeness he felt with her earlier, hearing the beating of their baby's heart. Whatever the reason he'd forget all about his differences with Sarah.

Just for tonight.

Nine

Sarah enjoyed the spicy gumbo, a warm mug of cider and the atmosphere at Smooth Tones. But more than that, she enjoyed feeling free…her celebrity going unnoticed. Being incognito was liberating, and only once in a while had she really worn her disguise to get out of her hotel when on tour.

She smiled at Code, and he smiled back.

He seemed to enjoy her anonymity, too. He was a man used to being behind the scenes, accustomed to secrets and security. So different from her life that was open to the whole world, not as much by choice but by situation.

Sarah leaned back and sipped her drink, the saxophone's sexy tunes drifting through the club setting a tempting mood of seduction.

"Dance with me," Code said, suddenly standing behind her and taking her hand.

Sarah rose and they walked hand in hand to the dance floor. Code held her waist and she roped her arms around his neck. They touched and swayed slowly with the indulgent music. She laid her head in the crook of his neck and breathed in his musky scent. Her senses reeled.

"I could get used to you being a brunette," he whispered.

A rippling chuckle escaped her throat. "Me, too. If it means that no one recognizes me."

"Maybe that's what I like the most," Code said, drawing her closer into his arms.

"Hmm," she mumbled, closing her eyes and letting the soft tones and her handsome husband sway her.

Code nibbled on her throat, tiny kisses that were the slightest feather touches. Goose bumps rose up and down her arms.

If only it could always be like this.

She moved her head slightly to gaze at him. He slanted his head at the same time, his eyes like sparkling deep blue flames, mesmerizing and enticing.

Her heart surged.

She loved this man.

She'd probably always known, but fear kept her from admitting it. Fear that he wasn't Cody any longer, but Code Landon, a shell of a man—hardened, cold and callous. Fear that he'd reject her and toss her aside. Fear that she'd broken his trust and she'd never regain it.

Tonight, he'd shown her his charming side to prevent her further sobbing, most likely. They'd chatted and laughed and truly seemed to enjoy each other's company.

He would tread lightly and walk on eggshells around her, she presumed, to keep the mother of his child healthy. She'd seen the look of pure awe and, yes, delight in his eyes when he'd heard their child's heart beating. She'd felt the same way, and love poured out of her.

That moment had been devastatingly sweet between them.

Sarah wanted Code to fall back in love with her. She wanted to smooth his rough edges and love him with all of her heart.

Did she dare?

What do you have to lose, Sarah?

They would end their marriage in divorce after the baby arrived. So all she really had to lose was her pride and her heart all over again.

Then and there, perhaps because she felt carefree and she loved being in Code's gentle arms, she decided, why not? Why not try to repair years of damage. Their child had everything to gain.

And so did she.

Sarah inched closer to him and tightened her arms around his neck. She looked up and spoke with a breathless whisper, "You're a great dancer."

He laughed. "You're lying."

She smiled and shook her head. "You haven't stepped on my toes once."

"Is that all it takes?"

"I remember you having two left feet in high school, Code. But now, you're darn—"

"I wasn't as bad as I made out to be. I wanted to get close to you."

"So you pretended to be a klutz at dancing?"

"Yeah, it was a ploy to get to know you."

Sarah stared straight into his eyes. "We did that, didn't we? We got to know one another?"

"I thought we did." Doubt crept into his eyes and his shoulders stiffened. "But I didn't really know yo—"

Sarah put a stopping finger to his lips. "Shh, don't spoil the night, Code. Please." Then she lifted up on tiptoes and brushed her lips to his.

She felt him relax, his mouth accepting hers and then he took complete control, wrapping his arms around her and bringing her up against him fully. He deepened the kiss, slanting his lips over hers and pressed her mouth open.

They danced and kissed this way, bumping into other couples on the jam-packed twelve by twelve parquet flooring until the music stopped.

Breathless, Sarah turned away from Code to applaud the band, trying to keep her wits about her, tapping down her complete joy at breaching his hard exterior.

Her nerves tingled with awareness.

Code stood behind her and she leaned against him as they listened to the bandleader. "We're taking a break. Be back in twenty. Drink, eat up, no reason you can't have fun until we return," he said in a deep Barry White voice.

Code whispered in her ear. "Let's go home."

Home.

Sarah never considered a hotel room her home, until now.

She nodded, and they exited the club quickly. The ride home was silent but for a few pleasured sighs that escaped Sarah's lips. Code held her hand throughout, and when they entered the suite, Sarah removed her wig and glasses, fluffing out her hair.

Code watched every move she made and the nearly tangible hunger in his eyes prompted her to take the steps to stand before him, open and vulnerable.

He took her breath away every time she looked

at him. Dressed immaculately, in a black shirt and trousers, his skin tanned and healthy, his eyes rich blue and so steady, Sarah wanted him. Her husband. The man she had always loved.

He reached out to catch a strand of her hair, curled it around his finger and stared at it a long time. Contemplative, his brows drew together. "The real thing is prettier than the wig."

She hoped so. "I thought you liked the wig?" she said softly.

"I liked what it represented, babe."

"What was that?"

"The girl I once knew."

"She's here, Cody. Standing right in front of you."

Sarah reached for him and planted a long, urging kiss to his lips. Code responded with a groan of desire, kissing her back and taking the lead.

His embrace brought her up against him, her thighs against his thighs, her desire pressed to his. She closed her eyes tighter when his erection strained between them.

"Oh, God," she breathed out.

Code gripped her derriere and positioned her into the juncture of his legs. They rubbed together erotically and Code bent his head to mouth her breast through the silky material of her blouse. Her nipple strained toward him, and he caught it with his teeth.

Her legs went weak. Her breaths huffed out rapidly. Her body burned for him. "I still love you, Cody," she whispered in a rush.

Instantly, Code's hands froze on her body and Sarah silently cursed her impulsive declaration. He stopped his seductive assault and lifted up, straightening his form to catch her heavy-lidded gaze and search her eyes. Then he set her away from him and shook his head. "No."

His Adam's apple bobbed up and down as he continued to stare at her. A tick worked the left side of his jaw. He stood stone still.

Dread entered her heart. What did he mean by no?

Didn't he believe her? Or was he warning her off?

His expression grim, Sarah's courage wilted fast.

"No," he repeated, then on an exasperated sigh, he commanded, "You should get to bed. It's late."

He walked out of the suite and left her standing there in the middle of the room, the Christmas lights sparkling vibrant colors against the penthouse windows, as Sarah's bright hopes faded quickly away.

Code sat at the Tempest bar nursing his second dirty martini, staring at the holiday greenery swooping down along the crown molding, an occasional ornament twinkling and catching his eye.

"You look like you could use some company." Betsy McKnight, Sarah's backup singer sat down next to him.

"Hi," he said, reluctantly. Code didn't want any company. He planned on getting royally drunk all by himself. He'd had to get out of that suite tonight and away from Sarah. She'd thrown him off-kilter with her pronouncement of love. The words reverberated in his head.

I still love you.

She hadn't spoken from the heart, he told himself. They'd been swept up in the moment. The entire night had been leading to their making love again.

He didn't want her love. That would complicate matters. He had a hard enough time keeping his hands off her. Believing she loved him would only spell disaster. Besides, lately her moods shifted like the wind due to her pregnancy.

But niggling thoughts kept entering his head. The conversation he had with Lenora had been an eye-opener. He'd had no idea Lenora's health had deteriorated to the point of losing her job when they lived in Barker. Seeing her in the wheelchair had been another eye-opener. Without the expert health and nursing care Sarah now provided for her mother, Lenora's life would have been a nightmare.

Code gestured for the bartender to come over then turned to Betsy. "What are you drinking?"

"Bailey's coffee," she replied to the man behind the bar. He nodded and walked off.

"I just spoke with Sarah," Betsy said. "A few minutes ago. She's confused."

"Yeah, well." He was about to say, that made two of them, but refrained.

"She told me you're married now."

"She must trust you." Code stared straight ahead. Frankly, he was surprised that Sarah told one of her band members their secret.

"I know about the baby, too, and I think it's fantastic. Congratulations."

He nodded and sipped his drink.

Betsy shifted in her seat to face him. "Sarah will make a great mother."

"Are you here to plead her case?"

"She's my friend, and I love her." The coffee was delivered and Betsy blew on it before taking a sip. "Actually, I think she's had a rough life."

Code grunted. Sarah was a huge success. She'd provided for her mother and sisters. She was loved by millions.

"Gillespie was a jerk. Brilliant in the business, but not good for Sarah." Betsy confessed, "I'm not sentimental. He needed to go."

"Amen to that." Code took a swallow of his martini, feeling somewhat justified in his aversion for the man. "Why do you feel so strongly about him?"

"He manipulated Sarah, and it took her ten years to see it."

"How?"

"He *made* things happen. I have my suspicions, but I'm keeping them to myself. All I came down here to say is that Sarah deserves a good life. And if you're the one to provide it for her, don't blow it."

Code's brows rose in surprise. He liked Betsy. She had spunk and audacity. "You don't hold anything back, do you?"

"Not my style." Betsy gulped down her coffee quickly and got up from the barstool. "I'm exhausted. These late nights and early rehearsals are getting to me. I'd better turn in. Thanks for the drink."

Code watched her leave, her words ringing in his ears.

He made things happen.

Code lifted out his cell phone and dialed a number. Before, Gillespie had just been a nuisance and none of his business, but now that he was married to Sarah, it was his duty to protect her and find out the truth.

He called the best man he knew for the job. "Hey, Johnson. I need you to drop what you're doing. I'm sending you to Nashville."

Sarah nibbled on her lip, pacing in the parlor, dressed in a sheer, flimsy white negligee.

"Go for it," Betsy told her just minutes ago, after her conversation with Code at the bar.

Sarah wanted a wedding night with her husband. She wanted to satisfy that hungry look in his eyes. She'd blurted out her love for him without thinking of the consequences. Code wasn't ready to hear her declaration without the explanations and apologies that went with it.

Sarah was ready to bare open her soul to him now.

And damn the consequences.

She had to ease her mind and conscience once and for all.

When she heard his footsteps approach the suite, she stiffened, her heart hammering hard against her chest. She almost lost her nerve and retreated into her own room, but she talked herself out of it. "You're not a coward, Sarah."

She stood her ground, and when Code entered, his shirt open at the throat, his day-old beard outlining his strong jaw line and his face taut with tension, Sarah stifled a groan.

"What are you still doing up?" he asked once he noticed her. Then his gaze flowed over her nearly naked body and immediate hunger entered his eyes.

She tilted her chin and she couldn't keep the haughty tone from her voice. "You ordered me to go to bed. I wasn't tired."

His shoulders sagged and he let out an impatient sigh. "Sarah."

"We need to talk, Code."

He approached her until they stood just inches apart. He lifted one layer of the gossamer gown and ran his fingers through it. "You expect us to *talk* with you wearing this?"

Sarah's face blistered with heat. She probably turned red as the proverbial tomato. He peered into her eyes, the midnight hue of his gaze penetrating hers.

With feigned bravado, she stared back at him. "I needed to get your attention."

"You've got it, babe."

Sarah inhaled a slow, deep breath and nodded. He'd given her the stage. "I never meant to hurt you, Code. I loved you with all of my heart. It's just that Robert made it all sound so simple, and I thought our love was strong enough to see us through. When you didn't write very often, my heart broke because I knew you got tired of waiting for me. I always meant for us to be together."

"You didn't write back. What was I supposed to think?"

"I meant to, but Robert was always pulling me in a hundred directions, and I didn't have any assurances for you. He kept telling me it'd be easier on you if I didn't give you false hope. He made promises that I would get the time I needed, but then my career just took off and I let him manipulate me. Mold me into someone that wasn't truly me. My ambition got in the way of everything. I didn't realize the regretful price I'd pay, and I'm so, so sorry."

She shook her head and tears welled up. "Mama was getting sicker by the day. We had no money for her medical treatments, much less providing for the twins. I couldn't turn down Robert's offer. It meant survival for my family."

Then she added, quietly, holding back tears, "I had all these dreams. For us. I thought I could do it all, Code. And instead, I lost you."

He put his hands in his pockets and looked down at the floor, nodding. "You lost me."

"Forever?"

Code snapped his head up and searched her hopeful eyes. She could almost see the battle raging in his mind.

She reached out to touch his shoulder, skimming her fingers up his throat to his chin. And further up to his mouth. He exhaled and blew warm breath slowly over her fingers.

"I want a wedding night with my husband. Is that too much to ask?"

He grasped her hand and pressed his mouth to her palm, kissing there, making all her nerve endings stand at attention. "Babe, that was a given, from the minute I stepped foot into the suite."

"Really?" She smiled at him, her joy overflowing.

"I can promise you a wedding night, Sarah. But that's all I can promise."

Disappointed, Sarah nodded. She understood. The time for talking was over. She'd said what needed saying and apologized to Code. It was the best she could do beside make love to him and hope he would forgive her one day. And begin to trust her again.

Sarah poured every emotion she held inside into her lovemaking with Code. While he was a man who took command, he relinquished his control, allowing Sarah to call all the shots. Sarah stripped off his clothes, teased him into a frenzy with her mouth then straddled him on his bed, gripping him tight and moving on him in slow, aching, delicious thrusts. He reached for her hips and guided her, his magical hands skimming along her sensitized skin.

Code's groans of pleasure spurred her to go deeper, absorb every ounce of him, gyrate until he huffed out her name in an anguished low rasp. She felt his utter surrender, the moment when she'd given him the utmost pleasure. He shattered and took her along with him, the climax long and powerful and beautiful.

Sarah flopped onto his chest and he held her in his arms while her breaths steadied and her sated body relaxed. She closed her eyes as he planted tiny kisses along her forehead, his hands weaving gently through her hair, and finally, she dozed.

She woke up spooned against Code, his protective arms around her tummy. She snuggled in deeper, scooting her backside against him and meeting with his fully aroused body. "Oh," she giggled. "Sorry."

"I bet you are," he said, playfully, his warm breath caressing her throat.

"How long did I sleep?"

"About an hour."

"Sorry."

"Don't be. You needed to rest. And after that workout, so did I."

Her giggle this time came out low and sensuous. Code didn't let it pass. He stroked her breasts, now extremely full and sensitive from the pregnancy. His touch elicited incredibly delectable sensations. She squirmed even more and met with his rock hard erection. "Whoops," she said.

"I hope you're well rested, because it's my turn now. And I plan to take my time."

Code didn't wait for an invitation—he rolled her onto her back and began his mind-blowing assault, his lips finding the most sensuous spots on her body. He kissed her on the mouth over and over, slid his tongue down her throat, nibbling, caressing, his hands roaming freely and playing with her highly responsive breasts. Her nipples pebbled hard as he thumbed then suckled them.

Sarah squirmed with pleasure. "Oh, Cody," she whispered in breaths that were barely audible. She arched her body, her hips rising and dipping with the ebb and tide of his slow deliberate ministrations.

And she fell deeper in love with him with each kiss, each stroke and each expert glide of his hands on her body.

He was a man's man, with a hardened exterior and one who commanded respect from all around him. But he was tender, too, and generous and so darn sweet when he wanted to be that Sarah refused to give up on him or their counterfeit marriage.

Code stroked the apex of her thighs, his fingers playing her like a well-toned instrument, and all rational thought flew from her head.

She surrendered fully to him, crying out in pleasure as he kissed her inner thigh and stroked her womanhood until she burned with crazy desire.

He took his time, and that drove her insane. When she wanted him to speed up, he slowed and drew out the pleasure until she panted and ached. "Code!" she pleaded.

"Hang on, babe. There's more."

"There couldn't be," she protested and his laugh was low and sexy.

He left that part of her body alone and continued on, stroking, caressing and nibbling until no part of her went untouched, unloved. Her skin reacted, her body hummed and her nerves went completely raw. He positioned her in many ways, teasing and tempting her with his magical hands and his perfect mouth.

Up on her knees now, he lay on his back and moved under her, gripping her hips and guiding her so that her swollen womanhood met his lips. She gripped the bed board for support.

And he suckled her, his tongue swooping in making her toes curl, her nipples tighten and her body pulsate. Slow, deliberate thrusts again. And again.

Sarah held on tight, in awe and wonder. The pain exquisite, he gripped her derriere from behind and held her to him relentlessly while he drew out every ounce of pleasure from her.

She felt the rise of her hot, blissful pinnacle, held on, held on, and then she erupted. Her senses overwhelmed, she sighed her pleas softly, erotically, the pleasure almost too much to bear. Her release was earth-shattering and mind-numbing and when she was completely through, Code lowered her down onto him, kissing her mouth and murmuring sweet words.

"You sing out your orgasm, sweetheart. Did you know that?"

Sarah's heart pressed against his. She didn't quite know where her heartbeats ended and his began. "I don't."

He kissed her hair. "You do, and it's a beautiful sight."

Sarah, fully aware of Code's rock solid body beneath her, wanted more. "You're a beautiful sight, too," she said, moving slightly off of him so she could palm his thick, hot erection.

Code stretched out fully on the bed, giving her access. "I'm all yours. Do what you want with me, baby."

Sarah smiled. "Let's see if I can't get you to sing, too."

In the morning, Code stood over the bed and watched Sarah sleep. Emotions he'd kept buried in his heart came rising up to the surface. She looked like an angel with all that long auburn hair splayed out on the pillow, and images of how devilish she'd been last night had him wishing he could join her back in bed.

But the last thing he'd wanted was to fall for her again. Her betrayal and his ultimate payback had been ten years in the making. He'd clung to it. He'd counted on it.

Sarah had gotten under his skin again. They were to have a child together, but he still didn't trust her. She had a blossoming career, a full life that didn't include him. He'd be a fool to love her again—no matter the past they had shared or the child they would bring into this world together.

Sarah opened her pretty green eyes and smiled, stretching her arms lazily over her head as she gazed at him fully dressed. "Where are you going, Code?"

Something powerful tugged at his heart. He needed to get away from Sarah and get a grip. "Willow Bend for a few days."

"Willow Bend?" Sarah sat up, dragging the sheet to cover the body Code had cherished all through the night. Her lips pulled down in a heart-shaped pout. "Why?"

Her disappointment angered him. He'd told her what to expect from this marriage. Did she think that seducing him would make a difference? Code hung onto his bitterness for dear life.

"I'm not the doting husband, Sarah."

A look of shock stole over her face. "What?"

"I warned you that I couldn't give you what you needed."

Her beautiful bare shoulders slumped. She blinked tears from her eyes and lifted her chin in haughty defiance, yet she couldn't conceal the look of complete dejection on her face. "I see you haven't changed at all, Code. Still a cold, uncaring bast—"

"Sarah, I never lied to you."

She brushed her hair off her face and stared him dead in the eyes, all sense of hurt gone. Now, she spoke through angry, clenched lips. "You want me to hate you, don't you? It makes your life much easier that way. I hate you, and you don't have to deal with your emotions. You write me off, and you don't have to admit that you're softer than you think. That maybe the Code Landon I knew back in Barker still exists, somewhere deep inside."

Code's temper flared. Damn her. She had a way of cutting right to the core. He reminded himself that she was the woman he'd married only to gain custody of his child. They would divorce soon after the child was born. She'd wronged him in the past, and just weeks ago she'd failed to tell him of her pregnancy. He wondered if she would have ever admitted to carrying his child if he hadn't found out by accident. She couldn't be trusted. It was better to keep his distance.

"I have to go," he said.

"You're not going, you're running."

"Wrong. I don't run away from my responsibilities. You do." He turned and walked out the door.

"You are now," she called out, and a soft thump hit the back of the closed door.

Code was sure she'd have tossed something more deadly than her pillow at him if she'd had the opportunity.

Ten

Sarah glanced in the backstage dressing room mirror and liked the image staring back at her. The glitz was gone. She could go onto that stage tonight singing a mix of Christmas songs and her biggest hits, feeling like herself again, Sarah Mae Rose from Barker, Texas.

She smoothed a curl back from her cheek and straightened her tan suede skirt. The only embellishments about her tonight were the subtle ruffles on her cream silk blouse and the scalloped embroidery on her nut-brown boots.

On a whim, Sarah reached into her jewelry case

and lifted her wedding ring out, staring at it with longing. Sentimental feelings washed over her and tears welled in her eyes. It was two days before Christmas and this was her last show. She'd raised an incredible amount of money for the Dream Foundation. She'd married the man she'd been destined to marry and was having his child.

But it was all wrong.

Code had been by her side all these weeks. He'd been attentive and patient. He'd seen to all her needs but he'd not given her the one thing she'd wanted most of all.

His love.

She'd had her wedding night with him, and it had been glorious, but since that time, he'd been cold and distant. At this point she didn't know if he had it in him to forgive her. She doubted he could ever love her again, but she was determined not to give up.

"I'm not the doting husband." She recalled his cutting words and sweeping sadness filled her heart.

She slipped her emerald wedding ring on her finger. "So pretty," she said, admiring the brilliant gem. "And I've hidden you away all this time." Sarah debated the wisdom of concealing her marriage and pregnancy to her family and to the world. She whispered, "Did I do the right thing?"

"No, you didn't." Robert's voice startled her and she whirled around in her seat.

"How'd you get in here?"

He smiled smugly. "Did you think you could stop me from seeing you, Sarah?" He walked into the small room. "I've stayed away to give you time to cool off."

"I don't need cooling off. I just got smart."

"You don't mean that, Sarah. If it wasn't for me, you wouldn't have had all this success. You would have been just another wannabe country girl. A *nobody.*"

"That wouldn't have been so bad." Sarah voiced her thought aloud. She loved to sing and had a gift for it, but she would feel just as satisfied singing in the church choir or in a local country band. The life she'd led had taken a toll on her and she'd come to realize that gradually from the sacrifices she'd made in her personal life.

"You're wrong, Sarah. You love the limelight and attention. You were born for it."

Sarah wouldn't give him the satisfaction of arguing. "What do you want, Robert?"

"You need me. I'm your manager, in case you haven't figured that out yet."

"I don't need you." Sarah rose from her chair and opened the door gesturing for him to leave. "I have a show to do."

Robert's face contorted and he sneered. "Don't dismiss me, Sarah. Are you forgetting that I know your secret?"

"Are you blackmailing me?" Sarah couldn't keep an incredulous tone from her voice.

He approached her by the doorway and took her hand. "That's a harsh word. Let's sit down and talk about this."

When he tugged, she resisted, but he wouldn't release her. Sarah's heart pounded, and her gut clenched with anger.

"Let her go." Code entered the dressing room and stood beside her. She gasped at his sudden appearance. She hadn't seen him since he'd left for Willow Bend.

When Robert hesitated, Code grabbed his wrist and yanked it away, then stood in front of Sarah.

"You again?" Robert's face flamed. "This is none of your business, Landon."

"Sarah is my business."

"Since when?"

"Code," Sarah intervened. "It's okay. I'm fine. Robert didn't hurt me."

"Miss Rose, you're on in three," the stage manager announced, popping his head into the dressing room.

Code glanced at her and nodded. "Go on. I'll take care of Gillespie."

"But—" Dread pulsed through her system. Code looked like a poisonous snake ready to strike. Robert Gillespie wasn't one to ever back down from a challenge. The combination meant trouble. But a little voice in her head told her that Code knew how to take care of himself. Heavens, the man oozed confidence, and no one ever got the better of him.

Not even her.

He urged again. "Go, Sarah. I'll take care of this." Code's eyes flickered with softness for a moment.

Reluctantly, Sarah left Robert and Code in the dressing room and greeted her audience, walking on stage to five thousand applauding fans.

Code closed the dressing room door and faced Gillespie. "Sarah doesn't need your services. She's made that clear. I don't want you bothering her again."

"Like I said, Landon. It's none of your business."

"I know all about you, *Robert*. Don't push me."

"You know nothing!" His pretty boy face flamed. "I molded Sarah Rose and made her the star she is today. She owes me, big time. I haven't threatened a lawsuit because Sarah can be reasoned with, but she broke our contract by firing me. I can make life very uncomfortable for her."

"I wouldn't advise doing that," Code said firmly.

"I'll do what needs doing. Including letting the world know that Sarah got knocked up! I'll go to the press. Let out your nasty little secret."

Code approached him, nose to nose. "No one threatens me or *my wife*. As long as I'm married to

Sarah, you'll never get your job back. I don't give a damn if you tell the whole damn world that Sarah and I are married and having a baby. Hell, you'll probably be doing us a favor. And her stock will probably go way up."

Robert's brows rose in surprise. "You're married?"

Code affirmed his answer with a nod.

"Damn you, Landon."

"Don't even think about causing Sarah any more trouble, you got that?" Code pressed his finger into Gillespie's chest. "I've got so much dirt on you, you'd need a shovel to get out from under it. I know you manipulated Sarah into leaving me in Barker. You made sure she never had time for me. I also know all of her 'dates' were orchestrated by you. You set them all up and made sure she was seen with the *right* people. Regardless of her feelings. Regardless if her association with them would cause a scandal. In fact, you hoped it would. Any publicity was good just as long as they spelled her name right."

Gillespie shrugged it off. "That's what a manager does, Landon. You're naïve if you think that's news."

"Maybe not, but you see, I also know something that will insure Sarah never setting eyes on you again. Something that could land you in jail."

Gillespie's eyes darted back and forth, contemplating what Code actually knew about him. Code relished the panicked glare he witnessed. He had Gillespie just where he wanted him. He played his hunch. "You see, I know you paid that man to attack Sarah on stage back in Nashville. Her career had slowed down. Things weren't going your way, so you manufactured an incident and scared Sarah half out of her mind for the publicity. For that alone, I should—"

Code held himself back from jamming his fist into Gillespie's face. His investigator had only minor clues about Robert's part in that onstage attack, but Code's instincts told him it was true. Judging from the desperate look on the manipulator's face now, Code had been right. He landed the final blow. "I have proof."

Gillespie's cocky demeanor changed, and deep frown lines appeared on his face.

"What, no denial?"

Gillespie shook his head. "You can't possibly have proof."

"And that guy my security team carted out of here the other night? You know, the man who rushed onto stage to get to Sarah? Well, he wasn't shy about giving details. You paid him to do it. And you paid two other men to deliberately create a disruption in the audience pretending to be in a drunken brawl, which brought my team to the opposite end of the concert hall. Then your man jumped on stage. You wanted Sarah frightened again so she'd lean on you for help. She'd look to you for protection. That's how you always operated, keeping Sarah in your emotional debt. Only, your plan backfired this time."

Gillespie's shoulders slumped, and he started for the door. Code grabbed his arm.

"What do you want?" he asked.

Code looked straight into his eyes. "You'll leave Sarah alone from now on. She's having my child, and I don't want her upset. Agree that you'll never see her again, and I won't go to the police and tell them what I know."

Gillespie's face fell with defeat. "Agreed."

Then he walked out the door and Code let go a deep breath. His hunch paid off, and his bluff worked.

Gillespie was out of Sarah's life forever.

Code followed Gillespie from a distance, making sure he got in his car and left the premises. He was glad the man was out of Sarah's life for good.

Code tucked his hands in his trouser pockets and walked back slowly toward the Harmony Room deep in concentration. From outside the concert hall, he heard Sarah's voice drifting throughout the first floor lulling the hotel with her sweet melodic tones.

Then the music stopped suddenly.

Sarah's voice cut off.

Code heard the audience's loud mumbling and thought it strange. His first thought was that the electricity had gone out—the music had stopped that abruptly. But the audience murmurs increased to a fevered pitch, and Code picked up his pace. Three men from the hotel's medical staff rushed by him. He caught up to one of them. "What's going on?"

"Someone collapsed on stage."

The uniformed medical technician ran on ahead as Code took it in, his heart racing with dread. He swore and began running, too.

Sarah.

By the time he entered the Harmony Room, paramedics and his security team surrounded the victim, keeping her safe from onlookers who had breeched the stage. The whole scene appeared surreal, but Code's one thought was to get to Sarah.

He ran onto the stage and shoved his way through the crowd, pleading to God for her safety. Suddenly, everything cleared in his mind.

"Hey, watch it," one of the medical technicians ranted until he recognized him. "Oh, sorry, Mr. Landon."

Code finally made it through the first responders and bent down next to the victim. He blinked and blinked again.

"Sarah?"

Sarah was kneeling beside her downed backup

singer, Betsy McKnight, holding her hand. "I'm here, Bets. You fainted. They think from dehydration. You're going to be okay."

Betsy smiled faintly up at Sarah and closed her eyes. "Oh God, this isn't the way I wanted to stop the show."

Sarah laughed, although Code witnessed fear in her eyes for her friend. "You're a show-stopper, Bets. But it's okay. No one will forget this concert."

"Let us through now, Miss Rose." The paramedics ushered Sarah and all others away as they settled the transport gurney by Betsy's side. "We'll take her to the hospital now."

"I'll go with her," Sarah said.

Betsy shook her head. "No, you finish your Christmas show, Sarah. I'll be fine."

Code's heart nearly tripped over itself with relief. Sarah was okay. His wife looked fit as a fiddle. The baby wasn't in danger.

Sarah spoke with the stage manager to make an announcement to the audience that the show would resume after a short intermission.

After they wheeled Betsy off the stage, Code reached for Sarah's hand. "We need to talk," he said, looking deep into Sarah's gorgeous grass-green eyes. He guided her off-stage to a secluded alcove and didn't waste a minute.

Backing her against the wall, he kissed her senseless. "Do you know how scared I was when I thought you were the one who'd collapsed on the stage?"

"The baby's fine," Sarah said, putting a protective hand to her belly, looking a little puzzled at his outburst of emotion. "I'm taking good care of her."

"Her?"

She smiled. "Or him."

Code blew out a breath and raked a hand through his short, cropped hair. "When I thought you'd collapsed, it hit me. Suddenly. I couldn't bear to have anything happen to you."

She searched his eyes and spoke slowly. "Because... of...the...baby."

"Because *I love you*," Code announced and then repeated the words more softly. "I love you, Sarah Rose. I've never stopped loving you. All these years, I couldn't move on with my life. Because of you."

Sarah's eyes sparkled. "I never thought I'd hear you say that again."

"I'm saying it. And I mean it. I love you."

"I love you right back, Code."

"Cody," he corrected and witnessed a grin spread across her face.

"I thought nobody called you that anymore."

"You're the only one. Are you good with that?"

Sarah touched his cheek gently, her face beaming with joy. "I'm good with that."

"I want out of our divorce agreement. I want you

to be my wife for real and forever. Are you good with that, too?"

"*So* good with that," she said without hesitation. "It's what I've dreamed about for years. You and me. And our baby."

"Yeah," he said.

"Miss Rose? Sorry to interrupt, but are you ready to finish the show?" the stage manager asked, stopping just short of the corner alcove. "The announcer already assured the audience that Betsy is going to be alright and that you'd finish your performance."

Sarah glanced at Code and he nodded his encouragement for her to go on.

She took his hand. "Come out there with me," she said, tugging him along. Code would have followed her to the moon and back if she'd asked.

Sarah didn't have to quiet the audience once they reached the stage. All eyes were focused on Code, the man Sarah brought onto the stage. She lifted the mike off the stand and spoke to her fans. "Guess I'll just add to the excitement tonight," she said with a chuckle. "I'd like to introduce you all to my wonderful husband, Code Landon. We're expecting a baby next year."

The audience erupted with applause and shouts of congratulations, and when the crowd settled down, Sarah went on. "He's been generous enough to match your donations from these past concerts. All proceeds will go to the Dream Foundation here in New Orleans."

Another round of applause broke out.

Sarah glanced at her husband with pure love in her heart. They'd been given a second chance, and she was certain nothing and no one would separate them ever again. "And I've decided that this will be my last concert for a while. I'm going into the mommy business."

Code tugged her into his arms and planted a sweet, loving kiss on her lips. "Are you sure?" he asked, his hand covering the microphone to block out his words to the audience.

She nodded her answer without blinking an eye.

"When you finish your performance, I'll be waiting for you."

Sarah watched Code walk off stage with a wave to the audience and stand on the sidelines. She knew she made the right career decision. It had been a long time coming and now that she had a future to look forward to with Cody by her side, she wouldn't pass it up again.

"You know, I haven't written a song in a long time," she said to her fans, "but this one…this one I wrote for my husband."

Although at the time, she hadn't realized the song was meant for Code, the lyrics flowing so easily that night. "It's called, 'Your Hometown Girl is Finally Coming Home'."

The band started playing and Sarah sung the ballad straight from her heart, pouring out each sentiment with deep devotion and love. She glanced at Cody in the wings watching her and found trust and love and the promise of a happy future in his midnight blue eyes.

With joy and hope surrounding them now, they'd been given a wonderful gift.

Christmas just didn't get any better than this.

* * * * *

Don't miss the last book in Suite Secrets,
RESERVED FOR THE TYCOON,
available February 2009
from Silhouette Desire.

Here is a sneak preview of
A STONE CREEK CHRISTMAS,
the latest in Linda Lael Miller's acclaimed
McKETTRICK *series.*

A lonely horse brought vet Olivia O'Ballivan
to Tanner Quinn's farm, but it's the rancher's
love that might cause her to stay.

A STONE CREEK CHRISTMAS
Available December 2008
from Silhouette Special Edition.

Tanner heard the rig roll in around sunset. Smiling, he wandered to the window. Watched as Olivia O'Ballivan climbed out of her Suburban, flung one defiant glance toward the house and started for the barn, the golden retriever trotting along behind her.

Taking his coat and hat down from the peg next to the back door, he put them on and went outside. He was used to being alone, even liked it, but keeping company with Doc O'Ballivan, bristly though she sometimes was, would provide a welcome diversion.

He gave her time to reach the horse Butterpie's stall, then walked into the barn.

The golden retriever came to greet him, all wagging tail and melting brown eyes, and he bent to stroke her soft, sturdy back. "Hey, there, dog," he said.

Sure enough, Olivia was in the stall, brushing Butterpie down and talking to her in a soft, soothing voice that touched something private inside Tanner and made him want to turn on one heel and beat it back to the house.

He'd be damned if he'd do it, though.

This was *his* ranch, *his* barn. Well-intentioned as she was, *Olivia* was the trespasser here, not him.

"She's still very upset," Olivia told him, without turning to look at him or slowing down with the brush.

Shiloh, always an easy horse to get along with, stood contentedly in his own stall, munching away on the feed Tanner had given him earlier. Butterpie, he noted, hadn't touched her supper as far as he could tell.

"Do you know anything at all about horses, Mr. Quinn?" Olivia asked.

He leaned against the stall door, the way he had the day before, and grinned. He'd practically been raised on horseback; he and Tessa had grown up on their grandmother's farm in the Texas hill country, after their folks divorced and went their separate ways, both of them too busy to bother with a couple of kids. "A few things," he said. "And I mean to call you Olivia, so you might as well return the favor and address me by my first name."

He watched as she took that in, dealt with it, decided on an approach. He'd have to wait and see what that turned out to be, but he didn't mind. It was a pleasure just watching Olivia O'Ballivan grooming a horse.

"All right, *Tanner*," she said. "This barn is a disgrace. When are you going to have the roof fixed? If it snows again, the hay will get wet and probably mold…"

He chuckled, shifted a little. He'd have a crew out there the following Monday morning to replace the roof and shore up the walls—he'd made the arrangements over a week before—but he felt no particular compunction to explain that. He was enjoying her ire too much; it made her color rise and her hair fly when she turned her head, and the faster breathing made her perfect breasts go up and down in an enticing rhythm. "What makes you so sure I'm a greenhorn?" he asked mildly, still leaning on the gate.

At last she looked straight at him, but she didn't move from Butterpie's side. "Your hat, your boots— that fancy red truck you drive. I'll bet it's customized."

Tanner grinned. Adjusted his hat. "Are you telling me real cowboys don't drive red trucks?"

"There are lots of trucks around here," she said. "Some of them are red, and some of them are new. And *all* of them are splattered with mud or manure or both."

"Maybe I ought to put in a car wash, then," he teased. "Sounds like there's a market for one. Might be a good investment."

She softened, though not significantly, and spared him a cautious half smile, full of questions she probably wouldn't ask. "There's a good car wash in Indian Rock," she informed him. "People go there. It's only forty miles."

"Oh," he said with just a hint of mockery. "*Only* forty miles. Well, then. Guess I'd better dirty up my truck if I want to be taken seriously in these here parts. Scuff up my boots a bit, too, and maybe stomp on my hat a couple of times."

Her cheeks went a fetching shade of pink. "You are twisting what I said," she told him, brushing Butterpie again, her touch gentle but sure. "I meant…"

Tanner envied that little horse. Wished he had a furry hide, so he'd need brushing, too.

"You *meant* that I'm not a real cowboy," he said. "And you could be right. I've spent a lot of time on construction sites over the last few years, or in meetings where a hat and boots wouldn't be appropriate. Instead of digging out my old gear, once I decided to take this job, I just bought new."

"I bet you don't even *have* any old gear," she challenged, but she was smiling, albeit cautiously, as though she might withdraw into a disapproving frown at any second.

He took off his hat, extended it to her. "Here," he teased. "Rub that around in the muck until it suits you."

She laughed, and the sound—well, it caused a powerful and wholly unexpected shift inside him. Scared the hell out of him and, paradoxically, made him yearn to hear it again.

* * * * *

Discover how this rugged rancher's wanderlust is tamed in time for a merry Christmas, in A STONE CREEK CHRISTMAS. In stores December 2008.

Silhouette

SPECIAL EDITION™

FROM *NEW YORK TIMES* BESTSELLING AUTHOR

LINDA LAEL MILLER

A STONE CREEK CHRISTMAS

Veterinarian Olivia O'Ballivan finds the animals in Stone Creek playing Cupid between her and Tanner Quinn. Even Tanner's daughter, Sophie, is eager to play matchmaker. With everyone conspiring against them and the holiday season fast approaching, Tanner and Olivia may just get everything they want for Christmas after all!

*Available December 2008
wherever books are sold.*

SPECIAL EDITION™

Kate's Boys

MISTLETOE AND MIRACLES

by *USA TODAY* bestselling author
MARIE FERRARELLA

Child psychologist Trent Marlowe couldn't
believe his eyes when Laurel Greer, the
woman he'd loved and lost, came to him for
help. Now a widow, with a troubled boy who
wouldn't speak, Laurel needed a miracle from
Trent…and a brief detour under the mistletoe
wouldn't hurt, either.

Available in December wherever books are sold.

THE ITALIAN'S BRIDE
Commanded—to be his wife!

Used to the finest food, clothes and women, these immensely powerful, incredibly good-looking and undeniably charismatic men have only one last need: a wife!

They've chosen their bride-to-be and they'll have her—willing or not!

Enjoy all our fantastic stories in December:

THE ITALIAN BILLIONAIRE'S SECRET LOVE-CHILD
by CATHY WILLIAMS (Book #33)

SICILIAN MILLIONAIRE, BOUGHT BRIDE
by CATHERINE SPENCER (Book #34)

BEDDED AND WEDDED FOR REVENGE
by MELANIE MILBURNE (Book #35)

THE ITALIAN'S UNWILLING WIFE
by KATHRYN ROSS (Book #36)

HPE1208

REQUEST YOUR FREE BOOKS!

2 FREE NOVELS PLUS 2 FREE GIFTS!

Passionate, Powerful, Provocative!

YES! Please send me 2 FREE Silhouette Desire® novels and my 2 FREE gifts (gifts are worth about $10). After receiving them, if I don't wish to receive any more books, I can return the shipping statement marked "cancel". If I don't cancel, I will receive 6 brand-new novels every month and be billed just $4.05 per book in the U.S. or $4.74 per book in Canada, plus 25¢ shipping and handling per book and applicable taxes, if any*. That's a savings of almost 15% off the cover price! I understand that accepting the 2 free books and gifts places me under no obligation to buy anything. I can always return a shipment and cancel at any time. Even if I never buy another book, the two free books and gifts are mine to keep forever.

225 SDN ERVX 326 SDN ERVM

Name	(PLEASE PRINT)	
Address		Apt. #
City	State/Prov.	Zip/Postal Code

Signature (if under 18, a parent or guardian must sign)

Mail to the Silhouette Reader Service:
IN U.S.A.: P.O. Box 1867, Buffalo, NY 14240-1867
IN CANADA: P.O. Box 609, Fort Erie, Ontario L2A 5X3

Not valid to current subscribers of Silhouette Desire books.

Want to try two free books from another line?
Call 1-800-873-8635 or visit www.morefreebooks.com.

* Terms and prices subject to change without notice. N.Y. residents add applicable sales tax. Canadian residents will be charged applicable provincial taxes and GST. Offer not valid in Quebec. This offer is limited to one order per household. All orders subject to approval. Credit or debit balances in a customer's account(s) may be offset by any other outstanding balance owed by or to the customer. Please allow 4 to 6 weeks for delivery. Offer available while quantities last.

Your Privacy: Silhouette Books is committed to protecting your privacy. Our Privacy Policy is available online at www.eHarlequin.com or upon request from the Reader Service. From time to time we make our lists of customers available to reputable third parties who may have a product or service of interest to you. If you would prefer we not share your name and address, please check here. ☐

SDES08R

nocturne™

New York Times bestselling author

MERLINE LOVELACE

LORI DEVOTI

HOLIDAY WITH A VAMPIRE II

**CELEBRATE THE HOLIDAYS WITH TWO
BREATHTAKING STORIES FROM
NEW YORK TIMES BESTSELLING AUTHOR
MERLINE LOVELACE AND LORI DEVOTI.**

Two vampires, each wary of human relationships,
are put to the test when holiday encounters blur
the boundaries of passion and hunger.

Available December wherever books are sold.

www.eHarlequin.com
www.paranormalromanceblog.wordpress.com   SN61801

COMING NEXT MONTH

#1909 THE BILLIONAIRE IN PENTHOUSE B—
Anna DePalo
Park Avenue Scandals
Who's the mystery man in Penthouse B? She's determined to uncover his every secret. *He's* determined to get her under his covers!

#1910 THE TYCOON'S SECRET—Kasey Michaels
Gifts from a Billionaire
He's kept his identity under wraps and hired her to decorate his billion-dollar mansion. But when seduction turns serious, will the truth tear them apart?

#1911 QUADE'S BABIES—Brenda Jackson
The Westmorelands
This sexy Westmoreland gets more than he bargained for when he discovers he's a daddy—times three! Now he's determined to do the right thing…if she'll have him.…

#1912 THE THROW-AWAY BRIDE—Ann Major
Golden Spurs
A surprise pregnancy and a marriage of convenience brought them together. Can their newfound love survive the secrets he's been keeping from her?

#1913 THE DUKE'S NEW YEAR'S RESOLUTION—
Merline Lovelace
Holidays Abroad
Initially stunned by her resemblance to his late wife, the Italian duke is reluctant to invite her to his villa, but it doesn't take long for him to invite her into his bed.

#1914 PREGNANCY PROPOSAL—Tessa Radley
The Saxon Brides
She's the girl he's always secretly loved—and is his late brother's fiancée. When he learns she's pregnant, he proposes—having no idea she's really carrying *his* baby!

SDCNMBPA1108